THE MIDWIFE'S DREAM

VICTORIAN ROMANCE

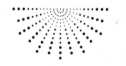

JESSICA WEIR

SWEETBOOKHUB.COM

WELCOME TO MY VICTORIAN WORLD

I am delighted that you are reading one of my Victorian Romances. It is a pleasure to share it with you. I hope you will enjoy reading my books as much as I enjoyed writing them.

I would like to invite you to join my exclusive Newsletter. You will be the first to find out when my books are available. Join now, it is completely FREE, and I will send you The Foundling's Despair FREE as a thank you.

~

You can find all my books on Amazon, click the yellow follow button, and Amazon will let you know when I have new releases and special offers.

Much love,

Jessica

CHAPTER ONE

"You look a little pale today," Kathryn Barton said as she reached out to lay her hand on her mother's forehead. "You're perspiring, are you..."

"Kathryn, stop! It's not polite to point out such things, what if your father heard you?" Beth Barton was in the last weeks of her confinement. With a look that bordered on fear, she peered over Kathryn's shoulder as if her husband might appear at any moment.

"Papa is at work," Kathryn said and laughed. "If he isn't concerned by his wife's health, then the shame is his, not mine."

"Kathryn! You mustn't!" Beth's voice had dropped to a whisper.

"He's in the city, Mama."

"But your sister is not!" Beth hissed. "You will upset her by saying such things about your father."

"Very well, but I still think you're pale and clammy. I think I ought to call the doctor."

"You know what your father will say. He doesn't like you learning this sort of thing."

"I'm going to have to learn such things if I want to be a nurse, aren't I?"

"You are just fourteen; there's time enough for you to think about such things in the future."

Beth was a little dismissive and it hurt Kathryn. She knew her father couldn't care less about educating women for work in any way, shape, or form, but she had thought her own mother might be on her side, at least in private.

"I'm hungry, Mama!" Jane, just twelve years old, sauntered listlessly into the room.

"Have you finished the work Miss Marlon set you?"

Beth asked in a tone that was more indulgent than it was stern.

"Yes," Jane said and sighed. "Although, I don't see the point."

"The point of being at least a little educated?" Kathryn scoffed; she and her younger sister were like chalk and cheese. Two more different sisters could hardly be found in all of London.

"When I'm married, I won't need to know how many degrees make up a triangle. Who even cares about such things?"

"Education is a privilege, Jane." Kathryn shook her head in exasperation. The sisters had had this same argument time and time again, with neither one giving an inch.

"For you, perhaps." Jane snorted with laughter. "Since no man will ever marry you!"

"If it's a man who wants an ill-educated woman, then I would sooner never be married!"

"Just as well!" Jane stuck out her tongue and then turned her nose up, signalling that she had won.

"Girls!" Beth's voice raised. "I'm tired and I cannot cope with your constant arguing." Already, their mother was walking away, heading for the stairs.

This was a signal that Beth was going to lay down on her bed. Lately, it seemed like all she ever did. Kathryn loved her mother dearly, but she often secretly wished that the woman had just a little more spirit. Of course, she was heavy with child and her fatigue was entirely understandable. However, with child or not, this seemed to be Beth Barton's way of doing things. She retreated. She gave in. She never, ever fought.

"Mama, I do wish you'd let me fetch the doctor," Kathryn persisted.

"And what would your father say?" Beth paused, her foot already on the bottom step. "He would remind you that we are not made of money!"

"We are far from poor, Mama." Kathryn shook her head. Her father's little sayings were both patronising and irritating to her.

"Because your father is careful with his money. He works hard, we cannot fritter away the proceeds of that hard work." And with that, Beth continued up the stairs.

The words were not her own, a fact which irritated Kathryn all the more. She'd heard these things word for word from her father's lips almost daily, year after year. He acted as if his own family were draining him. As if they had no right to be fed and clothed and live under his roof, even if that roof had only become his as a result of his marriage to Beth.

Still, her mother and Jane seemed to idolise him, for all the good it did them, for he no more favoured them than he did Kathryn, his errant daughter who insisted on thinking for herself. Kathryn, for her part, was glad to receive no favour from him. He was a selfish man who, in her opinion, if not her mother's and sister's, was entirely dissatisfied with his life. If ever a man regretted his choice of wife or the fact that his only children were female, it was Warren Barton.

"I'm still hungry," Jane said, but it was quietly spoken, not meant for their careworn mother's ears.

"Go down to the kitchen and speak to Mavis," Kathryn said, trying to let go of their differences for a moment. "She'll give you some bread and butter to keep you going until lunch." Jane smiled and nodded before disappearing from the room, leaving Kathryn alone.

Kathryn picked up the book she'd been reading the day before and sat down on the comfortable chintz-covered couch with a sigh. She was too distracted to read, but she opened the book to the correct page before setting it down on her lap. She seemed to be the only member of the household who was worried about her mother. Even Beth herself seemed not to care about her own health, as if she really were no more than a piece of equipment; a manufacturing unit producing babies, *or not*, as was so often the case.

Beth Barton had conceived no less than seven times to Kathryn's certain knowledge. All seven had been female, and only two of them survived. Kathryn wondered if her mother carried the much-coveted male now, or if a healthy child was to be just another female-shaped disappointment for her father.

She had come to despise the man who had arbitrarily decided that his entire family was pointless without a son. And if her mother managed to birth a healthy baby this time, and a male, no less, Kathryn wondered how she would feel about the helpless baby boy.

Would he grow up to be arrogant and dismissive? A chip off the old block, learning his habits and snarling opinions from his father? Or would he be his very own man? A fine man who would love and care for his mother and sisters, treating them as beloved, always listening, understanding, and never, ever assuming himself to be their better. Kathryn snorted, knowing the latter to be almost entirely unlikely.

CHAPTER TWO

"*P*oor Mama," Kathryn said quietly in the darkness.

"And poor Papa," Jane added, making sure that their father was protected, even amongst themselves in the dead of night.

"I hadn't realised you were still awake," Kathryn said, wishing she hadn't spoken aloud in the first place. She was listening to the arguing voices drifting through the still of the night, trying to make out the words through the deadening insulation provided by the walls of their three-storey terraced house.

"How could anyone sleep through Mama's crying?"

Jane said without a hint of caring or respect for their mother.

"Then perhaps Papa shouldn't be so cruel as to make her cry," Kathryn snapped back, irritated by her sister's ever-present position of coming down on their father's side. She sometimes thought of her mother and sister as whipped dogs, eager to do anything to please their master. Well, Kathryn would never be anybody's whipped dog, never!

"He just wants a son, Kathryn. Is that too much for a man to ask?"

"You are parroting his words, Jane. Do you never listen to yourself when you speak? Do you never wonder how it is Mama feels when she is so berated?"

"Other women have sons, Kathryn."

"At twelve you are so sure of life, aren't you?" Kathryn said, employing a little of her father's derision and noting how Jane bridled. So, she would only stand it from their father, would she? "How do you imagine you might feel one day to be in Mama's shoes? To have lost so many babies is heart-breaking

9

for a woman, and certainly not something she should be blamed for."

"I didn't say she should be blamed for that!"

"Oh, but she should be blamed for giving birth to girls? Really! Listen to what you're suggesting and try to educate yourself." Kathryn was angry now. How could they be so different? "If you understood anything at all of simple biology, then you would know that there is no way for anybody, man or woman, to ensure the sex of a child in the womb."

"The way you speak!" Jane made rather a good job of pious outrage. "If Papa heard you speak that way, he would punish you!"

"Biology is a fact of life, Jane. Understanding it might well spare you some agony in your future. It might make your choice of a husband something you think about very carefully, for one thing."

"Are you suggesting our father is not a good man?" Jane always fell on distraction when she had no sensible answer.

"No, I'm not. I'm not suggesting it, I'm saying it outright!"

"You selfish, ungrateful girl!"

"Again, you are parroting his words. For heaven's sake, Jane, learn to think for yourself."

"Why? So that I can be like you?" Jane scoffed. "So that I can read unsuitable textbooks and think myself clever? And for what? To end up as a nurse at St Thomas'? No, thank you!"

"You speak as if there's something shameful in it!"

"Shameful or not, Papa will never allow it, so who's the real fool here?" Jane's cruel, sharp tongue was well developed for a girl of just twelve.

"Go to sleep, Jane," Kathryn said with a sigh and covered her head with her feather pillow. Jane continued to talk, but Kathryn couldn't hear it. What was the point of conversation in such a house?

Still, Jane's words had cut her deeply, for there was some truth in them. Truth, at least, in her declaration that their father would never allow Kathryn to follow her dream of becoming a nurse.

Warren Barton was a curious mixture of conflicting ideas, but not uncommon in his contradictions. Like so many other men of their class, he chose to bemoan his lot, to belittle his family for the fact that he alone was the breadwinner. At the same time, his aspirations were so great that the idea of his daughters choosing a vocation of their own, of bringing some money into the household, was anathema to him.

How could a girl in such a household ever win? Perhaps Jane was right; perhaps Kathryn really was the fool. Jane was playing the game, never in conflict, always with her toe right on the line. Kathryn's determination to be herself, to follow her own dreams, to treat her life as her very own, had, she was forced to admit, caused her an endless amount of suffering.

Kathryn was always fighting, even though she fought in silence. She was always planning, always trying to escape the fear, the certain knowledge, that all her planning was in vain. Wasn't she just, in the end, making her own life miserable?

Knowing that she wouldn't sleep, Kathryn came out from beneath the pillow. Jane was mercifully silent, although likely still awake herself.

"You are no sort of woman at all!" Kathryn heard her

father's voice clearly and winced at the thought of her mother having to suffer his abuse. "For if you were truly a woman, a real woman, I would already have a son. I strongly suggest, if you know what's good for you, that you provide me with a healthy son this time, Beth."

Kathryn blinked back her tears, for they would be of little use. No wonder her sister thought that the sex of a child could be decided at will if their own father espoused such views. She hardly knew whether to pity her sister for being so blind or to be angry with her for being so determined to believe such a thing.

More than anything, however, Kathryn wondered what would happen if her mother gave birth to another baby girl.

CHAPTER THREE

"Just take it, Kathryn, I'm tired of arguing with you!" Beth said, sighing as she eyed her oldest daughter with undisguised exasperation.

"But Jane wants to take Papa his food!" Kathryn objected. "Why not let her?"

As was so often the case, Warren Barton had forgotten the wrapped midday meal which Mavis, the kitchen maid, had prepared and left on the dining table for him to pack into his briefcase. It happened so often that Kathryn had come to suspect he left the food there on purpose. He liked his family to run around after him. She knew he had the sort of petty personality which would enjoy the

14

idea that either his wife or one of his daughters would be forced to turn out in any weather to traipse through the London streets to the offices of Pirbright and Fullingham Investment Brokers in Westminster.

The family lived in Lambeth, on Cleaver Square. It was a fine place, not wealthy, not poor, but good for Lambeth. The houses on the street were a mixture of terraced brick-built homes in varying sizes. Some were so large that a houseful of servants was necessary. Others, homes such as the one the Barton family lived in, were much smaller, needing only a kitchen maid and the full attention of the female members of the family in keeping things straight.

Kathryn knew her father was envious of those living in the larger, servant-filled homes on the square. Of course, he never once looked beyond his little oasis of comfort to the swell of Lambeth poverty that was so evident just a matter of yards away. Never once was he grateful for what he had.

"I'd love to go, Mama. It's a fine day and Papa would be more pleased to see me than he would be to see Kathryn."

"Yes!" Kathryn said, choosing not to argue against her sister's petty snipe on this occasion.

"Jane has work to do! Miss Marlon is sitting alone in the drawing room with nobody to teach! Your father pays for this tuition, Jane, and I must insist you return to it at once." Beth was uncommonly firm.

Kathryn noted how she had chosen just the right bar with which to lever her youngest daughter back to her studies; her saint of a father was paying for it!

Jane shrugged but left the room, heading back to the drawing room where her tutor awaited. Beth stared at the paper-wrapped bread and cheese on the table. Mavis had left it in the centre of the table, clearing away everything around it. The very sight of it was enough to have Kathryn's blood boiling. What a selfish man, so pompous and demanding.

"Perhaps we should start putting Papa's food in his briefcase for him, that way he won't continually forget it." Kathryn knew she was prodding a hornet's nest, but she couldn't help herself.

"Oh, no," Beth said, seeming panicked. "No, your father wouldn't like that."

"Because he likes *this*. Because he does this on purpose."

"Kathryn!" Beth objected. "Not because he does this on purpose." Beth looked over her shoulder as she so often did, expecting her husband to have suddenly materialised. "Because he has important papers in his case and he wouldn't want us disarranging them."

"Mama, even you do not look convinced by your words."

"I must forbid you from interfering, Kathryn. You must promise me now never to mention a word of this or to touch your father's belongings in any way. You must promise me."

"Mama, of course." Kathryn softened. Her mother looked almost afraid and it made her feel guilty. Her own persistence had caused this. "I wouldn't do that." She reached out and touched her mother's arm as if to reassure her.

She had heard snippets of the awful things her father said to her mother, those disembodied words, fragments of sentences, drifting through the walls of their house at night. But what about all the things she *didn't* hear? How awful must those things be that

17

her mother would become so upset by the idea of the vaguest suggestion that narcissism, not forgetfulness, played the larger part in this weekly ritual of having his food delivered to him?

"Please, just take it to him," Beth said in a quiet voice.

"Of course." Kathryn picked up the packet. "I'm sorry, Mama," she added gently. "I just get cross with him sometimes." That, she knew, was an understatement of immense proportions.

"You mustn't. He's your father; I know he is not perfect, but he's still the head of this household. We rely on him for everything, and I cannot have you doing or saying anything which would put that in jeopardy." Although her words were quietly spoken, there was chastisement in them, a chastisement which Kathryn felt keenly.

"Jeopardy? Mama, why would anything at all put us in jeopardy?"

"Not us," Beth sighed. "Just please do not upset your father. He is in enough of a state about this child." She laid a hand on her swollen belly.

"He's worried it'll be a girl, isn't he?" Kathryn said and wished her tone wasn't quite so accusatory.

"He just wants a healthy child, that's all."

"Of course," Kathryn said. Once again, she knew that neither she nor her mother believed that.

Kathryn felt moved by her mother's plight, knowing that Beth was helpless to change anything in her world. Ordinarily, Kathryn distracted herself by determining never to find herself in such a position. Now, however, she put herself in her mother's shoes, and it felt awful.

Fearing that she might cry, Kathryn quickly kissed her mother's cheek and picked up the paper parcel of food. She smiled before turning to leave the room, hurrying away as the first of her tears fell.

For the first time in a long time, Kathryn felt truly sorry for her mother. She always privately took her mother's side, but it wasn't often that she did so without at least a little exasperation. This time, to allow herself to feel what her mother must feel was a most uncomfortable position indeed.

CHAPTER FOUR

*I*t was a cold but bright spring morning, the sort of day to make Kathryn forget all that troubled her, at least for a little while. The surprising tears had dried, and she found she was actually pleased to be out of the house now, despite her earlier protestations.

As cynical as life within the Barton family had made her, her rush of emotion that morning reminded Kathryn that she was still herself underneath it all. She still cared for her mother, it still hurt to be faced with the truth that there was nothing Beth could do about her circumstances. She couldn't control her husband, no more than she could control the outcome of her latest pregnancy. Kathryn tried to imagine her mother's feelings of helplessness and finding herself almost overwhelmed, shook her head and turned away from the pain of it.

As she walked along the long and seemingly endless Black Prince Road on her way to the River Thames her mind would not let it go. There was a fear inside her when it came to the child her mother was expecting. For all that she thought herself immune to her father's influence, still, she silently prayed for a healthy baby boy if only to spare herself, her mother, and her sister the inevitable suffering that would ensue otherwise. That she should hope for him to get his own way in everything made her feel useless, pointless, and she marched all the faster in an attempt to outrun so shabby a feeling. Squeezing the bread meant for her father's midday meal seemed the only way of exercising just the smallest amount of control of her own life. It was petty as things went, but it would do for now.

At the end of Black Prince Road, Kathryn paused as she always did. With the sun shining, the water of the River Thames looked cleaner, brighter. On a grey day, it always looked so murky and she was surprised how a fine day could somehow make the river and the London surrounding it look truly impressive.

Turning right, she headed along the embankment towards Westminster Bridge. The offices of Pirbright and Fullingham were on the north bank, she would have to cross the bridge to deliver his meal.

Ahead of her, just before the bridge, was the building which filled her every waking daydream and had done for so long, St Thomas's Hospital. The very sight of it took everything else away. The sadness, the helplessness, even the bright beauty of the day. Everything paled, everything faded.

Kathryn slowed her step, staring up at the building, never once doubting that she would one day walk its many wards and corridors, the proud recipient of some of the finest nurse training in all of England. This was where she always imagined herself, this was where she wanted to be. Kathryn could hardly remember when she had decided that to be a nurse would be the finest thing that life could offer her. She knew she had been very young, but for the life of her, she couldn't remember where that inspiration had come from. She couldn't remember the moment of deciding, the moment of feeling a vocation calling to her. How could something she felt so strongly have such seemingly vague beginnings?

By the time she reached the bridge and began to cross the river, her thoughts were already returning to her father, the man who was just minutes away from her now. The office he worked in was small, and she knew that there was very little hope of her not encountering him for a moment or two. If only she could open the door and throw his bread and cheese in without having to spare him another moment of her own precious life.

Kathryn wanted to go back, to retreat, to remember the feeling of looking up at St Thomas's Hospital. She stopped abruptly and turned on her heel, staring over at the hospital for just a brief moment before a young man who had clearly not expected her sudden change in direction collided with her.

"I'm sorry," they both said at the same time, and then Kathryn shook her head laughing.

"No, no, it was my fault, I changed direction."

"And I didn't look, I wasn't paying attention," the young man said, smiling at her and clearly determined to have no argument with her whatsoever. "But since you seem so willing to accept the responsibility, perhaps I might ask why you changed your mind so suddenly." His smile became more of a mischievous grin.

Kathryn couldn't help but laugh. "You'll think me very silly, but I wanted to look at the hospital."

"At St Thomas's?" he said and looked at her doubtfully. "Oh, dear, do you have somebody you care about inside?"

"Oh, no, nothing like that," Kathryn said brightly, struck by how curious and yet uplifting this little encounter was. "It's just that I'm going to work there one day." How did she manage to sound so confident of a future that her own logic ought to tell her was not assured?

"As a nurse?" he asked and seemed both interested and impressed all at once. How gratifying to have just one person in all the world provide an ounce of encouragement, even if that person were a complete stranger.

As Kathryn nodded enthusiastically, she studied the young man. He was tall and broad and a few years older than her. He was perhaps twenty, twenty-two at the most, but he had such bright and fresh features that he might have passed for a little younger. He had hair that was neither blond nor brown, being a very pleasing shade somewhere in between the two, and his eyes were a pale green, the black pupils standing out almost startlingly against the faded irises. He was a handsome young man, and if her head hadn't been so full of the hospital, so full of his encouragement which she saw almost as an endorsement of her hopes and dreams, she might have been a little flustered, a little shy and embarrassed.

"Yes, as a nurse," she said proudly.

"Well, if I'm ever sick, I certainly hope you'll be there to look after me." He smiled, nodded, and then continued on his way.

"So do I," she whispered to his departing back. "So do I."

CHAPTER FIVE

*H*er mother's piercing scream had Kathryn awake in a heartbeat. She sat bolt upright in bed, trying to steady her ragged breathing for a moment before coming to her senses and fighting to free herself from her twisted sheets and blankets. As soon as she swung her legs over the side of the bed, she reached out and turned up the oil lamp.

"Kathryn?" Jane said, looking at her quizzically and yet knowing all at once.

"It's all right, Jane, it's all right," Kathryn said, surprised by how steady her voice sounded as she sought to soothe her sister. "It's just Mama's time, that's all. Everything will be all right; you just stay here, and I'll go and see if there's anything I can do."

"All right," Jane said, looking up at her sister with fearful eyes. It wasn't often that Jane acquiesced, and Kathryn knew it was an accurate marker of just how afraid her young sister was.

Pausing only to slide her feet into her slippers and wrap a shawl around her shoulders, Kathryn dashed from the room. She hadn't lit a candle and had left the oil lamp in the bedroom to save leaving her sister in the dark. However, she could see light coming from under the door of her parents' bedroom, and it was enough of a marker to guide her safely down the long corridor.

She tapped gently on the door just as her mother cried out again. Not waiting for a response, Kathryn pushed open the door and made her way inside. Her father was pacing up and down the room, his hands on his hips in an almost irritated fashion. Her mother was lying on her side, trying to prop herself up on her elbows but seeming not to have the strength. Dashing past her father, Kathryn rushed to her mother's side and quickly set about making her more comfortable.

"Have your waters broken, Mama?" Kathryn asked, pulling back the sheets and looking for any sign. Her question drew a sharp look from her father, a look of disdain, but Kathryn ignored it. This was no time to play the part of a delicate young lady who knew nothing of the world. Of course, it was also no time to stride up and down the bedroom as if the timing of the baby's arrival was an inconvenience.

"Yes," Beth said weakly. "I think so."

Kathryn nodded in confirmation and then looked to her father to see if he was going to do anything at all to help.

"Papa, we need the midwife," Kathryn said, hoping to force him to some action.

"She's only just started, Kathryn," he responded in a superior tone. "These women charge for their time and I'm not made of money."

"But, Papa, given that it has not always gone well for Mama, perhaps it would be best."

"What do you know about it?" he snapped angrily.

"Forgive me, I am not trying to make you angry, Papa, I'm just trying to help."

"Then do something to help, girl, instead of telling me what you think I should do!" he said, and with that, he took his heavy dressing gown down from the hook on the back of the door, put it on, and strode out of the room.

"I need a midwife, Kathryn," Beth said weakly. "Something doesn't feel quite right," she went on, her face white and her eyes wide with fear.

"I'll go and fetch her, Mama." Her mother responded with nothing but a howl of pain. "I'll get Jane to sit with you while I'm gone."

Jane sat on a chair some distance from her mother's bed looking terrified. Kathryn was torn between feeling sorry for her and feeling angry with her, for how could she not care and have concern for her own mother at this moment? As young as she was, how could she put her own feelings first?

"Hold Mama's hand, Jane," Kathryn said in a voice which brooked no argument. "You'll need to move your chair closer." Jane did as she was told, but she didn't look at all happy about it.

As Kathryn ran back to her own bedroom to hurriedly dress, she felt suddenly alone. Her father and sister had abdicated any responsibility in this situation, leaving every decision to her. She was nearly fifteen, but suddenly she felt so much younger. She felt like a child who wanted to curl up in her mother's lap and ask what she should do next. But that mother, that source of comfort in the world, was relying on her now.

As soon as she was dressed, Kathryn ran down the stairs into the hallway, reaching for her cloak. As she wrapped it around her, the door to the drawing room opened and her father marched towards her.

"Just what do you think you're doing?"

"I'm going for the midwife," Kathryn said in the sort of tone that would have ordinarily earned her some physical punishment. This time, the man simply glared at her. "Mama is in pain and she has a great sense that things are not right. She needs somebody with the right sort of knowledge to help her."

"Aren't *you* the one who thinks herself a great nurse?" her father said in a horribly mocking tone that had no place given the current circumstances.

"For heaven's sake, Papa, I might well want to be a nurse, but I am not one yet. And I'm not a midwife, so I am not going to stand idly by and watch my mother suffering!" She had never spoken to her father this way before and it was, at that moment, likely the only thing which spared her. He was so stunned by her aggression that he stood as still as a statue, his mouth falling open, his eyes widening.

Kathryn took the opportunity to open the door and let herself out, slamming it behind her and running off into the night before he could catch her.

CHAPTER SIX

*J*anet Baldwin, a woman in her middle 30s with so many children that Kathryn didn't know where to begin counting them, was not at all pleased to be woken in the dead of night. As much as Kathryn tried to hurry her, the rough, gruff little woman seemed determined to take her time.

"Mrs Baldwin, my mother really is in a great deal of pain," Kathryn said as she watched the midwife slowly gathering herself.

"Birth *is* pain, girl," Janet said and snorted. "Never knew a birth that wasn't painful. If you find one, you be sure to let me know, because it will be a first."

"What I'm trying to tell you is that my mother thinks something isn't quite right."

"I've had a lot of experience with this sort of thing, so you let me be the best judge of that."

"With the greatest of respect, so has my mother. In fact, she's had rather a lot of experience of things going wrong."

"I will be ready when I'm ready!" Janet said, beginning to lose her patience.

For a moment, Kathryn hated the woman. Having given birth to so many herself, surely, she must know exactly how it felt to be waiting for help to come. There was, however, nothing that Kathryn could do or say to hurry her along. There was only one other midwife in the area who sat firmly in the price range that her father had decreed, and that woman was elderly and recently retired. Janet was an untested midwife in the Barton household, but she was all that was available to them. If only her father were a decent man, a good man who cared enough about his wife not to simply choose some rough little woman from Kennington Road. One, who could likely not even read and write, never mind have any formal training. Why did the man's decision have to be based on fiscal concern alone?

Of course, there were many midwives who didn't have formal training who were exceptionally good, but her irritation with this woman was bringing out the snob in her. But what good would snobbery do when her father refused to pay for anyone better?

When they finally arrived at Cleaver Square, Kathryn was relieved that there seemed to be no sign of her father in the entrance hall. No doubt he was back in the drawing room nursing a large glass of brandy, bemoaning his lot, annoyed that his sleep had been disturbed. He strove for respectability, and to a large degree, he had achieved that aim. He was firmly inserted in the middle classes, albeit the lower middle classes, and no doubt many of the lower orders looked up to him. But Kathryn, for as long as she drew breath, would never look up to that man. He had the appearance of goodness without an ounce of it in his heart.

"Follow me, Mrs Baldwin," Kathryn said gently, not wanting to irritate the only person who was able to help them now. "As soon as you're settled, I'll see to some refreshment for you."

"Very kind, I'm sure," Janet said, seeming pleased for the first time that night. Perhaps Kathryn should have made the offer of refreshment as soon as she'd knocked on the Baldwin's door; it might have made the awful woman move a little faster.

Kathryn knew that she would have to see to the refreshments herself, for Mavis Baines, the kitchen maid was just one more woman who didn't like to be given orders. If only her father would pay better, they would be better served. But Kathryn knew that her father only had a maid because a man of his station in life must be seen to have servants of some kind. If he did not, then he would have saved his pennies and been quite content to have his wife and daughters do everything.

When they reached her mother's bedroom, there was no sign of Jane whatsoever. Beth lay on her back, breathing hard and moaning, she was almost delirious.

"Right, let's get you onto your side," Janet said in an impressively business-like fashion. "And if you could get started with boiling some water, I'd be much obliged." She didn't even turn round to look at Kathryn.

"Of course," Kathryn said and hurried from the room.

She took a slight detour, heading for her own bedroom to find Jane. Her sister was lying on her bed with her head under her pillow. Kathryn, suddenly furious, pulled the pillow away from her to reveal Jane, silently sobbing and shaking, her face pale.

"Sorry, I just couldn't. I didn't know what to do."

"That's all right, Jane," Kathryn said, torn between wanting to comfort her and shake her. "But I need your help now. I need you to wake Mavis and the two of you set about getting water boiling. You can manage that, can't you?" she said gently, reaching out to take Jane's hand.

"Yes, yes, I can do that," Jane said, seeming relieved to have some part to play which didn't involve being anywhere near her mother. She didn't even seem to mind being the one who would have to wake the small, dark, aggressive Mavis Baines.

Kathryn followed her sister down the stairs and built up the fire in the stove, intent on supervising for just long enough to see that things were going smoothly in the kitchen. Once Mavis and Jane had things underway, Kathryn hurried back to the stairs. She paused at the door to the drawing room, placing her ear against the smooth painted wood. She cursed inventively under her breath when she heard the unmistakable sound of her father snoring. What a pig he was!

CHAPTER SEVEN

"*I* need you to keep pushing, Mrs Barton," Janet said some hours later when the baby had still not arrived. It was dawn, and Kathryn could hear the first of the birdsong as the black of night turned into the grey of early morning.

"I can't," Beth said, entirely exhausted. "It's just not coming."

"Mama, I'll help you. Hold my hand, squeeze it as hard as you like." Kathryn had repeated the same words over and over again for hour upon hour.

"We have to remember to make a list of everything we need for Christmas. We must make sure that we speak to the butcher and get a goose in good time this year," her mother said in a dreamlike voice.

Why was she talking about Christmas, it was long past?

"If you don't hurry up and give birth to this child, it *will* be Christmas by the time you're finished!" Janet said with little sympathy. "It's not the first time you've done this, it shouldn't be taking so long."

"Then perhaps we need a doctor, Mrs Baldwin," Kathryn said, having a heavy feeling in her gut, knowing as her mother had known earlier that something was not right. "We could do with a second opinion, some guidance."

"I've helped bring hundreds of babies into this world, I'll have you know!" Janet said mustering every ounce of indignation she could find.

"And what do you do if it isn't going well?" Kathryn asked, starting to feel helpless. "Do you never call for the doctor?"

"What do men know about birthing babies? Nothing, that's what, especially those that think themselves educated!" Janet was so far up on her high horse now that there would be no bringing her down.

"But if there's something wrong..."

"There's nothing wrong that a bit of effort wouldn't cure. Now come along, Mrs Barton, I know what I'm talking about. I've given birth to nine myself, and every single one of *mine* lived!" Janet threw her words carelessly but they came out as an accusation — as if Beth Barton was responsible for so many ill-fated births. If the awful woman wasn't the only help available, Kathryn would have cheerfully choked the life out of her.

"We'll have to get something a little nicer for Mavis this year. I don't think she liked her gift last year and this house is hard enough to run with her, I shouldn't like to run it without her," Beth went on, not even moaning now, seeming hardly to be aware that she was in the middle of giving birth. The delirium frightened Kathryn, and she had determined there and then to go and fetch a doctor herself.

However, just as she was getting to her feet, her mother almost rose to sit, and she screamed in agony.

"That's it, keep pushing!" Janet bullied. "Push, for goodness sake! Push!" Janet was shouting and Beth, her eyes wide, simply did as she was told. She seemed stunned as if to be in pain and in the middle of giving birth was the very last thing she had expected. She had been lost in a world of Christmas preparations, even in the spring, and now she simply looked shocked and terrified. Tears rolled down Kathryn's face; why could her father not have made better provision?

"Push!"

"Yes," Beth said meekly, taking a great breath, then pushing and screaming at the same time.

"Push!" Janet yelled again, and Beth did as she was told.

Kathryn had the greatest sense that her mother was pushing too hard, that even in childbirth that level of effort should not have been required. It was as if her mother was pushing against something that wasn't going to come, constricting it, stifling it.

"No, no," Kathryn cried out, sobbing now. "Something is wrong! You must stop pushing, Mama. You must wait until I have gone for the doctor."

"Never mind the doctor! This baby is coming now, look!" Janet said somewhat triumphantly.

When the baby's head appeared suddenly, Kathryn's mouth fell open. She had read and educated herself enough to understand the mechanics of childbirth, and yet nothing had prepared her for how utterly bizarre it looked. There was suddenly a child's face, purple and screwed up, where she might innocently have never expected it to be. And yet there it was, its eyes closed, its lips blue.

"What is that?" Kathryn said, forgetting the gory unreality as she advanced, staring down.

"It's a baby! What do you think it is?" Janet scoffed.

"What's that around its neck?" Kathryn bellowed angrily. "There's something around the baby's neck! Look, just look!"

Suddenly, Janet looked panic-stricken. She stood in an agony of indecision, looking one moment as if she might tell Beth to push again, and in another that she might tell her to stop.

"Mrs Baldwin, is that not the umbilical cord? Surely, it shouldn't be wrapped around the baby's neck?"

"You must run for the doctor, this minute," Janet said, her face pale now, all her bluff and bluster evaporated into thin air.

"But you must do something for the baby now!"

"The baby isn't far enough out for me to do anything. Now, run and get the doctor!"

Kathryn ran as fast as her legs would carry her, hoping that the doctor would move himself a lot faster than Janet Baldwin had. Still, the sun was beginning to come up now, and perhaps the doctor would already be out of bed.

As she ran, she sobbed, she was so out of breath that she felt sick. She despised her father, laying on one of the couches in the drawing room getting a full night's sleep. And her sister, suddenly so useless, so unable to help in any meaningful way. But then, what had Kathryn done? She had failed to stand up to Janet Baldwin. She had known something was not right, she had known they should have gone for the doctor. And now, in her heart, she knew it was all too late. She was running as fast as she could, even though she knew it was pointless.

Suddenly, she wanted to be more than a nurse, she

wanted to be a midwife, to spare women the treatment her mother had received. Would it ever happen? Would she have the courage to tackle such a perilous task?

CHAPTER EIGHT

arren Barton surprised his oldest daughter by not going out to work as he ordinarily would have done that day. Instead, he had sent Jane out of the house with a message to Pirbright and Fullingham that he would return the following day.

He sat at the breakfast table, as usual, eating his ordinary breakfast and saying not a word as Mavis Baines poured his tea. Mavis looked tired and resentful. There was not a hint of sympathy in those cold grey eyes. Kathryn, who stood at the table pouring hot water into a separate pot for her mother, thought what a fine pair they were, her father and the kitchen maid, both heartless and self-centred.

"Are you taking a tray up to your mother?" Warren asked, his voice rather flatter than his customary agitated tone.

"Yes," Kathryn said gently, feeling exhausted.

"Perhaps a little toast and butter might be in order," he went on, surprising her entirely. It was as close to kindness as she had ever seen him, and she instantly mistrusted it.

"Yes, I'll see if she can manage a little toast." Kathryn butted two slices of toast and cut them into quarters, arranging them neatly on the plate. She set the plate on the tray, hardly daring to make eye contact with the father she had so wilfully disobeyed the night before.

She had fully expected a volley of argument regarding the doctor and the extra expense, not to mention the fact that she had so openly disrespected him in the matter of going early for the hapless midwife. For all the good it had done any of them! Yet, so far, there had been nothing and it was making her nervous.

As Kathryn reached the stairs, Jane slipped silently in through the front door. Kathryn paused and turned to look at her sister, seeing that her eyes were red-rimmed from crying. She had no doubt that Jane cared about their mother, but she didn't have the courage needed to be able to support her in the worst of times. Perhaps she was to be the person who would forever boil the water and never be in the room.

"I'm going to take these up to Mama. Do you want to come with me?" Kathryn asked hopefully.

"No, I'd better go and check on Papa."

"He seems perfectly all right to me!" Kathryn said, unable to hide her anger. "After all, he's not the one who's just given birth to a dead child, is he?"

"But he has lost his only son! You know that all he ever wanted was a son, and now he has been denied it!" Jane said aggressively, although Kathryn was under no illusion. As much as the girl forever defended their father first, she knew that she was defending herself. She had done nothing to help her mother, and she couldn't hide the shame in her eyes for all her posturing.

"You defy words sometimes," Kathryn said and sighed before turning to make her way upstairs.

Kathryn entered her mother's room silently, setting the tray down on the bedside table and looking down, she seemed more unconscious than asleep.

Beth's face was drained of colour, barring the skin around her eyes which were so dark from crying that she looked as if she'd been struck. She'd lost a lot of blood, although the doctor had managed to stop the bleeding and help her deliver the baby — it would never draw breath in this world. Janet had stood meekly to one side. Kathryn had not even looked at her for fear that she would fly across the room and attack her.

She knew that the woman hadn't caused the fatal strangulation of the child who would have been Kathryn's baby brother, but she had allowed her pride to assure herself that she knew all there was to know about bringing babies into the world. She had refused to recognise the signs of a mother in distress, and she had refused to listen to Kathryn's pleas. She hadn't caused the baby's death, but perhaps she had allowed it.

Kathryn felt a bright spark of anger overtake her exhaustion. Women deserved better; babies deserved better. She had to get her training, she had to make a difference in the cold hours of pain that could bring either joy or despair.

Whilst the doctor had measured out a sleeping draught for Beth, one designed to keep her in a drowsy state for days on end, Kathryn had tidied up her mother and the bed alone. Janet had made to help her, but Kathryn couldn't bear it and had, instead, sent her downstairs to take payment from her father and then take her leave. When she had everything under control and the doctor had administered the first dose of the sleeping draught, he had told Kathryn that she would do better to get a little sleep herself. He seemed to understand without being told that the lion's share of responsibility had fallen on her young shoulders that night. She was so grateful for his silent recognition that her eyes had filled with tears, but she had not slept. Everything felt unreal, awful, and she had known there was no point in laying down.

"Kathryn?" Beth said weakly, fighting to open the eyes that were little more than slits.

"Could you manage some tea, Mama?"

"No, I don't think so, my dear."

49

"I do wish you would eat something, or at least drink something."

"I'm so tired."

"I know, Mama," Kathryn said and left the tray where it was, sitting down on the edge of her mother's bed and reaching out to take her hand. "I'm so sorry."

"You did everything you could. You never left me, my love, and I shan't forget that."

"I should have run for the doctor sooner. I should have known that something was wrong."

"I don't think there was anything he could have done. I think my boy had already gone. I could feel him leaving me, Kathryn, even as you ran for the midwife."

"Oh, Mama," Kathryn said and began to cry. Even if there had been nothing Janet Baldwin could have done, even if the baby boy had already died in his mother's womb, Kathryn would never forgive her for her arrogance. How many women in the world suffered at the hands of the ignorant masquerading as the knowledgeable?

"How's your father taking it?" Beth asked, the fear was evident even in her drugged eyes; her husband had yet to call into the room to see her.

"I do not care!" Kathryn said through gritted teeth.

"I wish you could understand how hard it is for me, Kathryn. I have my own heartbreak to contend with, but somehow the effect of your father's mood will always come first. I have never been able to do anything about that, and doubtless, I never shall."

"Mama, I'm sorry. I'm so, so sorry." Kathryn bowed her head and was surprised when her mother reached out and gently stroked her face.

"You've nothing to be sorry for. You did everything you could, and I do love you, my dear."

"I love you too, Mama. I love you more than anybody in the world."

As her mother drifted off to sleep Kathryn felt both fear and rage. Somehow, she knew that things were changing she just couldn't understand how, or what she could do about it.

CHAPTER NINE

or several days, there was no sign of the anger that Kathryn had been fully expecting. Her father remained quiet, and whilst he hadn't shown any particular kindness, he hadn't shown any particular cruelty either.

He continued to work as normal, setting off each day at the same time after a hearty breakfast at which he said very little. Beth, still suffering the effects of so difficult a birth and the subsequent heart-breaking disappointment, was keeping to her room. She ate very little, largely surviving on warm, milky tea, and Kathryn could see the weight dropping from her, leaving her gaunt-looking, older somehow.

For her part, Kathryn didn't trust the curious quiet.

She couldn't imagine that it would last, and she was already anticipating the day when the quiet would turn on its heel and leave. The day when her father would begin to berate her mother again, questioning her very womanhood, blaming her for the loss of her own child.

These were the thoughts which rolled around her mind as Warren Barton and his two daughters sat at the breakfast table that morning. He ate well, as he always did, the sound of his chewing and his folding and refolding of the newspaper he always read at the table in favour of conversation, irritated Kathryn as it had done for as long as she could remember.

He seemed for all the world as if nothing had happened, as if a child who should have been living and breathing in that very house had not died. It was as if the wife he had married, sworn to protect, sworn to love, did not even exist. Her misery did not extend beyond the walls of the room upstairs, the room he had quit on the night of the birth and never once returned to. How could he leave her up there alone? How could he let his wife lay there in torment and not give her one single word of solace, of care? All that he had lost was a matter of his own pride, his own determination to produce a son in his own likeness. But Beth had lost so much more. She had lost her baby, the child she had carried for month after month. Oh, how Kathryn despised him.

"Would you like something particular for dinner this evening, Papa?" Jane asked with forced brightness, her eyes big and pleading as she looked up at her father, reminding Kathryn of a beaten dog.

"Not really," he replied without looking up from his newspaper.

"I thought we would have Mavis make toad-in-the-hole, Papa. It's your favourite, isn't it?"

"All right then, we will have toad-in-the-hole," he went on, his voice flat and uninterested, his gaze still firmly fixed upon the financial pages.

Jane's smile gave her the appearance of being pleased, but the crestfallen look in her eyes told its own story. Kathryn pitied her; why couldn't the silly girl see that their father would never care for them? Why did she persist in trying to please him at every turn?

Finally, her father got to his feet and opened his briefcase, stowing his newspaper inside. Then, quite uncharacteristically, he reached for the wax paper parcel of food that Mavis had left on the table as she always did and stowed that in his briefcase also. So, it would not please him today to have one of his daughters cross Westminster Bridge to bring the King his luncheon!

"Have a good day at work, Papa," Jane said, her father simply turned to look at her and nodded vaguely. "We'll see you this evening."

"Yes," he said and picked up his briefcase and walked out of the room without looking back once.

The sisters sat in silence listening to the sounds of their father leaving; his footsteps drifted down the entrance hall, pausing as he put on his overcoat, and then the door opening, clicking quietly closed behind him.

"Oh, that man!" Kathryn said with a burst of anger as she slammed her hand down onto the table.

Mavis, who had clearly been waiting outside the dining room for her master to leave, sauntered in, her eyes on Kathryn. There was just the vaguest hint of amusement on her face as if there was something in Kathryn's angry outburst which gave her pleasure.

Something about it made Kathryn feel filled with doom. How could one survive in such a house? How could one hope to be normal? With a cruel father, a jealous and spiteful maid, a pathetically needy little sister, and a mother so heartbroken that she lay broken in tiny pieces wanting nothing but solitude?

Knowing that the moment Mavis had left the room her sister would make some sharp reply, Kathryn decided to make herself scarce. She wasn't in the mood to have yet another exasperating conversation with a little sister who always thought she knew better, and she didn't have the energy to spare with which to despise a belligerent kitchen maid.

Instead, she poured some tea, buttered some toast, and set off with a tray for her mother's room.

CHAPTER TEN

"*J*ust sit down and eat your dinner, Jane!" Kathryn said waspishly. Her sister had left the table and was standing by the window peering out into the street beyond. "It's getting cold."

"We cannot start dinner without Papa here," Jane said in a complaining voice.

"The dinner is already spoiled beyond recognition in the time we have waited for him, Jane. It is half-past eight, for heaven's sake! As Papa very well knows, we eat at seven. And we eat at seven, Jane, because our father decrees that we should eat at seven."

"You always have to be so nasty, Kathryn. He works

very hard for us, for that very meal in front of you now, the least you could do is wait for him to come home before you set about eating it. He is the head of this household, after all."

"Really? My goodness, I would never have guessed. Surely, the head of the household would have taken the reins a little bit tighter these last few weeks, would he not?"

"And just what exactly do you mean by that?"

"Does it not anger you, Jane, that our mother lays upstairs with her heartbroken, and our father has never once been up to enquire after her well-being?"

"Anger me? No, of course it does not!" Jane said defensively. "I'm sure she will be up and about soon."

"How would *you* know? When *you* barely see her, how on earth would you know that?"

"I have seen her!" Jane was still defensive.

"You really have no idea, do you?"

"And you do?"

"You have no idea what this last birth did to our mother, do you?"

"She has lost babies before. She has lost so many that it is no wonder our father despairs," Jane said looking a little haughty.

Kathryn was on her feet and advancing upon her sister before she knew what she was doing. All she could see was the child who should have been her brother, the umbilical cord wrapped around his neck, his face blue, his eyes dead. Upon reaching her sister, she slapped her hard across the face. Jane cried out, tears immediately rolling down her cheeks.

"If you had had the courage to be with our mother that night, you would have seen what I saw. You would have seen what I saw, and you would not stand there now defending a man who hasn't an ounce of caring or understanding for the wife who has suffered so much. Do you know what a dead child looks like, Jane? Do you know what a baby boy who has been strangled looks like?" Kathryn was so furious that she was shaking, but she knew she must get a hold of herself. Jane was younger, smaller, and no matter what she said, she did not deserve to be struck.

Kathryn was overcome with anger and regret all at once.

"Don't say such things, Kathryn. I don't want to think about it. I didn't want to see, and I don't want to know." Jane was crying in earnest and finally, giving in to her regret and letting go of her anger, Kathryn took her young sister into her arms and held her tightly. She was surprised when Jane returned the embrace wholeheartedly, clinging to her as a child might cling to its mother. She was sobbing, her thin shoulders shaking, and Kathryn realised she had never felt so low in all her life.

"I'm sorry, Jane. I should not have struck you; it was unforgivable."

"I just wish he would come back. I just wish I knew where he was."

"I know you do, and I'm sorry. I just cannot forget what I've seen. I cannot forget bearing witness to what our mother suffered that night. Her heart is broken, Jane. I don't think she can take any more, and I know that she will never be the same again. I know that you love our father dearly, but I do not. I suppose we ought to just agree to differ on that point.

I cannot make myself love him just as you cannot make yourself despise him. But we should not be at one another's throats, really, we should not. After all, with a mother laying upstairs unable to take part in life, and a father who is largely absent from the house, we really do only have each other."

"Yes, I know," Jane said, her sobs having died down, her thin body juddering only now and then.

"Unless, of course, we count Mavis," Kathryn said in a purposely flat tone.

"Oh, dear," Jane said, and her tears turned to laughter.

"That's better, that's better, my dear Jane." Kathryn kissed the top of her sister's head. "Now then, you need to eat something, we both do. What do you say we sit down and enjoy Mavis' glorious toad-in-the-hole, even if it *is* cold?"

"Yes, all right," Jane said, gently pulling away from her sister's tight embrace, casting one last forlorn look out of the window before crossing the room back to the dining table.

"And as soon as Papa comes in, we'll have Mavis

warm his food for him. We shall tell him that we didn't want ours to go to waste."

"I wonder when he'll be back," Jane said, returning to her initial concern, the very thing which had begun their argument in the first place. This time, however, Kathryn did not give in to her own spiralling despair.

"I'm sure he's just had to stay late in the office, Jane. Or perhaps he's having an hour or two in his club before he comes home. Either way, he'll turn up sooner or later, don't you worry about that."

"Yes, I'm sure he'll be back soon," Jane said and nodded, cutting into her food without an ounce of enthusiasm.

Despite her gentle words, however, Kathryn couldn't help but hope that the awful man never came back again. If he had fallen under the wheels of the carriage on his way out of his club, Kathryn knew that she wouldn't be able to find an ounce of care with which to mourn him.

CHAPTER ELEVEN

"*Y*ou've been so good to me, Kathryn."
Beth was sitting up in bed and
looking healthier than she had done
for many days. She wore a sad smile for her
daughter. "But it is too much responsibility for you.
It's time I face the world again. It's time I attended to
my own duties."

"Your only duty, Mama, is to get better. I really don't
think you're ready, not yet." Kathryn was playing for
time. It had been four days since she had seen her
father and she had yet to find the courage to tell her
mother about his absence.

"I need to get back into my life, my dear. You're

strong, but Jane is not. As your mother, it's my responsibility to make things right, not yours. The sooner this household returns to normal, the better it will be for you and Jane. I can't imagine that your father is very happy about me keeping to my room. No, it's time I pulled myself together." She looked so fragile that Kathryn could have cried.

How could she tell this already crushed woman that her husband seemed to have disappeared?

"You still look so pale, Mama. Give yourself another day or two at least, please," Kathryn implored.

"I can see in that pretty face of yours that there's something you're not telling me. You say that I'm pale, but I believe that you are more so. Your eyes look so dull, not their normal wonderful shining blue. So, perhaps now is the time for you to tell me."

Kathryn could hardly believe that her mother could tell so much from a look. She had given her the proper credit, assuming that her mother lacked an understanding of the world rather than realising that she simply lacked the opportunity to express herself as she otherwise might. Her father had taken her spirit, even when he was not there.

"There's nothing for you to worry about, really."

"You are treating me like a child, my sweet, I won't have it. I'm your mother, and I demand to know what is troubling you." Beth reached out and took Kathryn's hand. Realising that she had yet one more appalling responsibility upon her shoulders, tears began to roll down Kathryn's face.

She was beginning to wonder how much more she could take herself. A witness to the stillbirth of her baby brother was more than she could bear and yet she had needed to watch the suffering of her mother, and the cruel and irresponsible absence of her father, fifteen-year-old Kathryn Barton was beginning to feel very old indeed. And now, on top of it all, it was for *her* to break her mother's heart yet again.

"Papa has disappeared, Mama. Well, he hasn't come home for several nights. I'm sure he's only at his club, indulging himself, licking his wounds, whatever it is that man does whilst we struggle on alone without him. Please, you must not worry about it. You must promise me that you will not worry about it, Mama. You have suffered enough already without my father's selfish behaviour adding to your misery."

"He has gone? He has left us?" Beth was instantly in a state. Her pale blue eyes were wide and terrified, her hands clawing at the bedsheets as if to steady herself with them.

"He's probably just as his club, Mama. As I said, I'm sure there's nothing for you to worry about. You really must just concentrate on yourself." Even Kathryn wasn't convinced of what she was saying, and worse still, she felt guilty for ever having wished her father would never come back in the first place.

The truth was, that in her heart, Kathryn didn't care if she never saw the man again. In all honesty, it would suit her never to lay eyes on him. However, he was their stability, their security, and she realised that they would struggle to survive without him. Could this really be punishment for her own wicked thoughts? Did the world really work that way?

"I think I will stay here for a while," Beth said and began to slide down the bed, no longer determined to take the reins of her life as she had been just moments before. She disappeared beneath the covers, and Kathryn could hear her gentle sobs. How much more could this poor woman take?

Kathryn waited with her mother until she fell into a fitful sleep, exhausting herself after a full hour of crying. She made her way downstairs to find Jane perched on the couch in the drawing room, a book on her knee. A book she was looking at but not reading.

"I'll see if Mavis will make some tea, Jane," Kathryn said, feeling that weight of responsibility once again. She needed her father to come back, she needed her mother to come back to life, she couldn't do this all by herself.

"You'll be lucky if you can get her to listen to you now that Papa isn't here. Just you wait! When he gets back, I'm going to tell him every sharp remark that horrible girl has made. I'm going to tell him about every time she has ignored instructions and done just as she pleases! She'll be sorry, you see if she isn't!" Jane looked furious, but Kathryn could instantly tell that it was just a diversion from her deeper fear.

"He'll be back, Jane. I've no doubt that he is doing this to make Mama suffer, to teach her a lesson as if losing the baby was something she'd done on purpose. But he'll be back, he really will."

"Do you promise?" Jane looked at her with big, tear-filled eyes.

"I promise," Kathryn said, surreptitiously crossing her fingers behind her back. How could she promise that which she did not believe?

CHAPTER TWELVE

*T*he sunshine of the last days had deserted London, leaving it a grey and washed-out place. It was warm enough for a spring day, but miserable, nonetheless. Kathryn thought that it suited her mood well to have such dull weather, for dull was exactly what she felt.

She crossed Westminster Bridge slowly, not pausing to look back over her shoulder at St Thomas's Hospital as she so often did. The hospital and her life, her future, seemed so far away now, so impossible. Her head was filled with what the next few minutes might bring, what would happen when she reached the other side of the bridge and the offices of Pirbright and Fullingham.

Her father had been gone for a full seven nights now, and with the housekeeping money falling low and Mavis constantly complaining about how much she had to do with so little, the time had come for action.

Beth had retreated from her life again, still locked away in her bedroom, hardly eating, surviving on warm, milky tea. Jane was waspish, aggressive, lashing out left and right, privately blaming their mother for the absence of their father. And so, it was left to Kathryn to face him, to be the one to turn up at his place of work and ask him to come home.

By the time she reached the door of Pirbright and Fullingham, Kathryn was shaking. She felt hot and clammy, and her mouth was dry.

"Good afternoon," a young woman who sat at a desk by the door looking neat and prim, gave her a fixed smile. "How can I help you?"

"I am Warren Barton's daughter, Kathryn," Kathryn said, a little confused. Why on earth did the secretary look at her as if she had never seen her before?

"Yes, of course," the woman went on, beginning to look uncomfortable.

"I'd like to speak to my father, please. Would you be so kind as to tell him I'm here?" Kathryn said formally.

"I'm afraid he's not here, Miss Barton," the woman said, her cheeks flushing a little.

"Perhaps if you could check," Kathryn said somewhat sternly.

"I can assure you he's not here, Miss Barton." The woman's voice also grew a little stern.

"Can you tell me when he is due to return?"

"No, I'm afraid I can't."

"I would like to speak to Mr Pirbright, please," Kathryn said and began to walk past the woman's desk. Her mother and sister were suffering, and she was not about to be turned away by the sharp, neat young woman.

"I'm afraid Mr Pirbright is extremely busy today, Miss Barton. Perhaps you would do better to come back tomorrow."

"No," Kathryn said defiantly, turning her back on the woman and striding over to the door to her father's office. She rapped loudly on it and opened it, finding it entirely empty.

Not just empty of her father, but of anything that might suggest he still worked there. There was a desk, a chair, and a table lamp, but nothing else. There were none of the papers that she had previously seen laying all over his desk whenever she had been forced to deliver his luncheon.

The pen he was so proud of in its purpose-made stand had disappeared, as had the inkpot and blotter. Kathryn fought to understand what she was looking at, to find some context.

"As I said, your father is not here," the young woman said, although a little more gently this time.

"Where is he?" Kathryn asked, her voice low as she slowly turned to face the woman.

"Ah, Miss Barton," Mr Pirbright, obviously hearing the muted altercation from behind his heavy oak door, walked cautiously out of his office. "Perhaps we might have a little word in private, my dear." He waved an arm in the direction of the office he'd just vacated. Kathryn walked helplessly through the doorway. Everything seemed unreal as if she were in a dream and she had an awful sense of doom.

"Mr Pirbright, forgive me for interrupting your work, but I don't understand what's happening. Where is my father? Why does his office seem so empty?"

"I'm afraid your father doesn't work for Pirbright and Fullingham anymore, my dear."

"You have terminated his employment?" Kathryn asked in something of an accusatory tone.

"Oh, my goodness me, no," Mr Pirbright said, shaking his head so vigorously that his pince-nez shifted on his nose and he was forced to remove them before they fell off. "No, he left of his own accord. I believe he's gone to work for another firm."

"Another stockbroker?" Kathryn asked, her confusion so great that she began to feel physically numb.

"I imagine so," Mr Pirbright said, looking distinctly embarrassed.

"But which one? May I have the address?"

"I would gladly give you the address, my dear, if I

knew it." He sighed and swept a hand down over his eyes as if he had the beginnings of a headache. "Sit down, Miss Barton," he went on, and there was such a tone of pity in his voice that Kathryn began to feel sick and afraid.

"How can you not know?"

"Your father left us a little over two weeks ago, Miss Barton. He gave us very little indication, and it appeared that he had secured another position before leaving this one."

"But surely, he told you where he was going? I mean, he has worked with you for years, hasn't he?"

"Your sentiments are mine, my dear. I cannot pretend that I am happy about his conduct. He had never given any indication of being unhappy here at Pirbright and Fullingham, nor that he thought his conditions were in any way unfair. So, I am bound to admit that I was rather disappointed when he gave so little notice."

"And he didn't tell you where he was going?" Kathryn persisted.

"Forgive me, Miss Barton, but is this not information

that you ought to get from him yourself? I am surprised that he has not mentioned to his family that he has taken alternative employment."

"Mr Pirbright, I have not seen my father in seven days. He just didn't come home one night, and we haven't seen him since. At first, I thought that he might be staying at his club. I mean, after everything that happened, well... I mean..."

"I know, Miss Barton," Mr Pirbright said with gentle care. "I am aware of what happened and am very sorry indeed. I do hope your mother recovers quickly."

"And you say he left you a little over a fortnight ago?"

"Yes."

"Then it is something he arranged after my mother... After my mother lost..."

"I really am terribly sorry, Miss Barton. I wish that there was something I could tell you, something that would help."

"What would be the use?" Kathryn said, staring off into the middle distance as the full weight of her circumstances hit her like a steam train. "What would be the use when the man himself does not want to be found?" She lifted her face to look at him, but she could hardly bear to see the embarrassment and pity in his eyes.

"If there is anything I can do, you must let me know," he said, in that overtly caring way utilised by people who sincerely hoped that they would never be called upon for help of any kind.

"Thank you, Mr Pirbright. I will not take up any more of your time," Kathryn said and got to her feet, excusing herself from his office and making her way outside with as much dignity as her battered pride could muster.

What would they do now?

CHAPTER THIRTEEN

"There's a man at the door says his name is Mr Arklow," Mavis said solemnly, her cold grey eyes surveying Kathryn with thinly veiled contempt. Kathryn had never known exactly why it was Mavis didn't like her, but then Mavis Baines didn't seem to like anybody.

"Mr Arklow?" Kathryn said, nonplussed. "Did he say what he wanted?"

"I asked him, but he said he wasn't going to discuss it with a maid!"

"Very well, thank you, Mavis. Leave it with me, I'll go to the door."

Not for the first time, Kathryn felt the weight of responsibility. Although her mother was physically fitter than she had been for many weeks, she still kept to her room. She hadn't been out of it since the night she had given birth, and she seemed to Kathryn to be retreating further and further into her own world day after day. She had retreated so far, in fact, that she no longer asked if her husband had returned to them. The truth was that she barely spoke at all.

As for Jane, in the month since their father disappeared, she had become more and more angry, more and more difficult to speak to. That curious moment of closeness which had existed between them the first night their father had failed to return home had all but vanished. Nonetheless, Kathryn was careful not to let her anger overrun her as it had done so shamelessly on that night. Instead, she tried to remember that her sister was young and afraid, however combative she might seem.

"What can I do for you, Mr Arklow? My maid says you refused to state your business." Kathryn spoke with firm efficiency.

"*Your* maid?" he said, taking in her obvious youth.

"My mother is indisposed, Mr Arklow, and for the time being, the maid in this house works at my direction. I must say that you now have far much more information about me than I have about you, sir." She raised her eyebrows waiting for the man to finally state his business.

"Oh, dear, I do hope your mother is well, young lady."

"Miss Barton; Kathryn Barton." She was trying to thaw out her communication, even though this man's appearance on the doorstep was now starting to unsettle her.

"Well, Miss Barton, I am Matthew Arklow, and I work for Bowers and Klein chartered building surveyors."

"Indeed?"

"And we have been appointed by Mr William Montgomery to check over the property and make sure that there are no particular areas of improvement required which might have an effect on the sale price." He was looking a little bemused as if he couldn't quite understand Kathryn's confusion.

"The sale price?" Kathryn said, unable to hide her confusion. "What do you mean *the sale price?*"

"The price that Mr Montgomery has agreed to pay Mr Warren Barton in the event of a successful survey, Miss Barton. Surely, your father has made mention of it, my dear?" He was beginning to look less sure of himself. "I am assuming, of course, that Mr Warren Barton is, indeed, your father."

"He is," Kathryn said, and she could feel her cheeks flushing with shame. "But I am afraid to say that we have not seen my father for some weeks, and he has not informed us of his intention to sell this house."

"Then my appearance at your door must be a terrible shock, Miss Barton," Matthew Arklow said and cast his eyes down, looking truly regretful.

He was a middle-aged man, a few years older than her father, with a face that she could now see was rather kindly. He had let go of his professional facade for a moment and seemed as if he were quite ready to offer some comfort. Feeling a little lightheaded, knowing that she needed to sit down, Kathryn could do no more than invite the man in.

"Please," she said, stepping back and opening the

door wider, indicating that he should enter. He followed her through to the drawing room where Jane sat silently reading a book.

For more than two weeks, Jane had had no tuition from Miss Marlon, largely because household funds were beginning to run low and suddenly education had become much more of a luxury and much less of a right. Not, of course, that Jane minded very much. She always complained about her lessons and had seemed mildly pleased when Kathryn had been forced to have a most awkward conversation with the young tutor. Perhaps, one day, Jane might regret her reliance on a good marriage and her complaints about the education that so many other children would be grateful for.

"I really ought to speak to your mother, Miss Barton, but if, as you say, she is indisposed, I do feel I ought to give you as much information as I have. It seems only fair, my dear."

"Take a seat, Mr Arklow," Kathryn said, fighting hard to hold herself together. What did this mean? What did it mean for their future security?

"Information?" Jane said, sitting up straighter and looking suddenly bright. "About Papa?"

"Not really, Jane. I'll explain it all to you in a moment," Kathryn replied as gently as she could. How on earth was her sister going to take this news?

"Mr Arklow, do you know when my father put the house up for sale?"

"For sale?" Jane squealed.

"Jane, please, I must find out what's happening first. There will be time enough for this later, but I beg you, behave yourself."

"I really am so sorry; I feel as if I have thrown your entire household into turmoil."

"You are just the messenger, Mr Arklow, you have nothing to regret. But please, when did my father put the house up for sale?"

"I believe it was a little more than five weeks ago, Miss Barton."

"Five weeks?" Kathryn said, horrified to realise that her father had begun to sell the house before he had even disappeared, never once mentioning it to his family. She really was afraid now.

"Forgive me for my impertinence, Miss Barton, but have you searched for your father?"

"I have been to his place of work, a place he worked for many years, only to discover that he quit his position there and has moved on. Unfortunately, his previous employer was unable to tell me where he had gone."

"He refused?" Mr Arklow looked outraged.

"No, he just didn't know, my father never told him. I got the impression that he had rather let them down." She almost added *just as he let us down*.

"I don't really know the strict proprieties, professionally speaking, but perhaps it might help a little if I tell you the name of the solicitor your father is using for sale of the property. I've seen it on some documents, and in the circumstances, I feel I cannot leave this house without passing you that information. Although, I would beg you to keep my name out of things if you possibly can. As I said, I do not really know the strict proprieties."

"I would be very grateful, Mr Arklow. And I shall say nothing of how I learned the details, I promise."

"The solicitor's name is Mr Arnold Wolverton. I believe he works out of an office somewhere between Kennington and the Elephant and Castle. I don't know exactly where, but I could only imagine it would be somewhere on the main Kennington Road. At least it is not far from here, at any rate."

"Thank you, I cannot tell you how relieved I am to have at least that much information." In the face of all his kindness, Kathryn began to let go of the shame of abandonment. This was her father's shame to hold, not hers.

"I do hope you will forgive me, both of you, but I am expected to return to the office today with the details of my survey of your home. I really do feel awful about it." And he truly looked awful, remorseful.

"I understand, Mr Arklow. You may look around the house at whatever you need, but would it be truly necessary to go into my mother's room? I am going to have to find a gentle way to tell her all of this, and she is currently not in the best of health. I can assure you there are no defects to speak of and that the condition of the room is much like the rest of the house."

"Of course, Miss Barton."

"Would you like me to take you upstairs now and show you the other rooms? After that, you may wander about as you please." Kathryn was already on her feet.

"Thank you, really," he said and got to his feet also. "I truly am very sorry; I cannot imagine your suffering."

Kathryn dare not look at Jane as she led Mr Arklow from the room. She was grateful that he tiptoed up the stairs, obviously keen not to disturb her mother and become yet further embroiled in their family misery.

He made quick notes as he went, making short work of the survey of the upper floor of the house. Kathryn then took him downstairs into the kitchen where Mavis, sullenly pounding bread dough on the table looked up quizzically, scowling at the man who had refused to tell her his business on the doorstep.

Sooner or later, of course, Kathryn would have to tell

her. She couldn't begin to imagine that the sale of their family home heralded good times, and certainly not good enough to keep the one and only servant they had. But Kathryn couldn't think about that now; she just needed to show Mr Arklow around the house and let him leave. As kind as he had been, she wanted him gone. She wanted him gone so that she could let go of this temporary adulthood and return to the child she felt like on the inside. She wanted to throw herself face down on the floor and cry until there wasn't a single tear left.

CHAPTER FOURTEEN

*I*t was too late to visit her father's solicitor that afternoon, and she had cried so much that she wasn't fit to be seen out of doors. With her emotions overwhelming her, Kathryn knew that she would make little sense in any meeting with a solicitor, something in which she would be out of her depth on even the best of days. She just had no knowledge of such things, no experience that extended beyond her home, her education, and her dreams of a life.

Kathryn didn't look much better the following morning, but at least she had stopped crying and had managed to get just an hour or two of sleep. There wasn't time for her to wait to come to terms with all she'd learned, especially when there was so much more to find out. So much was unknown; so much hung in the air like dust motes.

Kathryn found the office of Mr Arnold Wolverton on Kennington Road, just as Mr Arklow had suggested. It was a small and somewhat shabby office, somewhere she had walked past countless times in her life and never noticed.

She peered in through the window and saw a white-haired man sitting at the desk, wire spectacles perched on his nose as he leaned over some papers. She gently pushed the door open and hovered, waiting for him to notice her. However, the man was most intent on his work, and so she cleared her throat loudly, closed the door, and advanced into the room.

It was a most untidy office, a far cry from the setup at Pirbright and Fullingham, the only other office she had ever been into. There were two desks, although there was only a chair at the one which the man, presumably Mr Wolverton himself, was sitting. The other desk was strewn with papers and, she could see quite clearly, undisturbed dust on every corner.

The wall behind Mr Wolverton was lined with heavy books, probably legal tomes, most of which looked like they had not been taken down for some time, given that the dust was equally undisturbed on the shelves. It came as little surprise to her that her father had come to an office like this for his legal work, given that this particular solicitor was likely to be a little cheaper than the others.

"Excuse me?" Kathryn said when the man still did not look up. "Are you Mr Wolverton? Mr Arnold Wolverton?" she went on.

"Oh, hello," the man said, his head snapping back in surprise. "Forgive me, child, I did not see you there!" he went on and smiled broadly.

His accent was so cultured, almost painfully upper class, and she could hardly imagine that a man whose breeding had been fine enough to furnish him with such a manner could work in such a shabby little place. He didn't seem to fit at all.

"Mr Wolverton?" Kathryn repeated.

"Yes, my dear." He was smiling at her with extraordinary friendliness, and if her heart wasn't so flattened, Kathryn would have been thrilled to meet this man. "Now, what can I do for you on this fine morning?"

"It is a little irregular, I believe, but I have a problem," Kathryn said, and then paused to give herself a moment or two to find the right words to describe her peculiar situation. "I live on Cleaver Square with my mother, father, sister. My father, Mr Warren Barton, has been missing for some weeks. I have searched for him and discovered that he no longer works in the office he once worked and that his former employers have no idea where he is working now."

"I see," Mr Wolverton said, clearly recognising her father's name but thankfully not looking suddenly cautious or guarded as she had expected he might.

"Yesterday, Mr Wolverton, a building surveyor came to our home unexpectedly. It was then that I discovered that my father is selling the house. I'm sure I ought not to be asking, but we have had no word from my father and have no idea what he expects us to do once our home is sold."

"He has made no mention?" Arnold Wolverton's eyebrows, bushy, grey, and curiously splendid, lowered. "He has said nothing of the arrangements he has made?"

"I do not even know where he is, sir. I would not ask, but I am aware that you are acting for him in this sale and would be very grateful for anything you can do for us. My mother would have come here herself, but she is terribly ill and has been since before my father left us. Mr Wolverton, is there anything at all that you can tell me?"

"I daresay there is a little information I can impart without being terribly indiscreet with my client's business. And given that he has failed to mention to me that he leaves behind a family who have no prior knowledge of the sale of the home in which they live, I daresay I do not mind being more open with you than I ordinarily might."

"Are we to be thrown out on the street, Mr Wolverton?"

"I will make contact with your father today, my dear, and find out exactly what his intentions are."

It gratified her to see that he now quite clearly viewed his client with a good deal of disapproval. Kathryn had certainly never needed an ally more than she did now.

"You know where he is then, sir?"

"I do know where he is, but I am afraid it is one of the things I cannot tell you. I wish I could; in fact, I cannot impress upon you how much I wish I could, but I cannot. However, I will most certainly make contact with you as soon as I have word from him, and I will make it plain that I am now aware of the curious situation he has left you and your family in."

"I cannot help thinking that he has left us for good, Mr Wolverton, and that it is rather cowardly of him not even to mention it."

"If that is indeed what he has done, young lady, then I am bound to agree with you. It is certainly not the actions of a fine man, but I am afraid that I'm not in a position to be too picky about my clients." He cast an eye about the room and gave an amusing grimace, once again igniting her curiosity as to how such a very obviously well-bred man had ended up working in such meagre surroundings.

"Thank you, Mr Wolverton." In the face of his kindness, Kathryn's eyes filled with tears. They were already rolling down her cheeks before she'd had a chance to even attempt to blink them back.

"There, there, child," Mr Wolverton rose from his seat and reached out a hand, patting her gently on the shoulder before opening the drawer of his desk and taking a fresh handkerchief from a neat little pile. Kathryn was diverted once again; how could he be so neat and fastidious in one area and not another?

"Thank you," she said, taking the monogrammed handkerchief from him and quickly drying her eyes.

"I shall call upon you at Cleaver Square either this afternoon or tomorrow. If you do not see me today, then take it that I have not managed to speak with your father. If I do not manage to speak to him by tomorrow, I will call upon you anyway to let you know. But trust me, my dear, I shall not leave the situation as it is." He shrugged. "Whilst I really am not in a position to be picky about my clients, some things really are beyond common decency."

"Thank you. I really am so very grateful."

As she walked slowly back to Cleaver Square, Kathryn found it hard to find any hope, even though she was certain that Mr Wolverton would find an answer for her. But answer or not, she was as sure as she could be that such new knowledge would only be a confirmation of her worst fears.

CHAPTER FIFTEEN

"*I* think Papa is just going to surprise us with a nice new house, a nice new start." Jane looked adamant, even if her frightened eyes gave away her true feelings.

"Jane, did you not listen to a word that Mr Wolverton said? Did you not hear him state very clearly that our father no longer wishes to live with us in the same house?"

"But what if Mr Wolverton has it wrong? He's so dishevelled and disorganised, I can hardly imagine that he gets anything right!"

"Now, that's enough!" Kathryn said, defending the ageing solicitor who had been so very kind to them.

"Mr Wolverton is Papa's solicitor, not ours. He didn't have to go out of his way to help us, and even if the news is not good, it is not his fault." A sense of exasperation and hopelessness was boiling around inside of her and she had to bite her tongue. "When will you take your blinkers off and see Warren Barton for the man he really is? When will you stop idolising him as if he were some kind of God? He is so far from it that it is laughable!" Kathryn spat the words angrily before taking a few deep breaths and reining in her temper once more. After all, Jane was going to suffer even more than she was. She was going to suffer more because she loved their father whereas Kathryn did not.

"Girls, please do not bicker, I cannot cope with it." Beth was almost slumped on the couch with a heavy shawl wrapped around her shoulders. It was the first time she had been downstairs since the night she had gone into labour, and she looked truly awful.

She had been in a great decline since it became clear that her husband had not simply disappeared for a night or two, but Kathryn had begged her to sit in the drawing room for at least long enough to hear what Mr Wolverton had to say. However, beyond listening, Beth had made no contribution to the conversation, she had simply stared vacantly into space as if she couldn't take another ounce of what life had left to throw at her.

"Mama, did you hear everything that Mr Wolverton said?" Kathryn wished that she were not the only person in the room willing to believe what was happening. She needed help; she needed their support. She couldn't do this on her own.

"He's gone," Beth said definitely. "He's gone and he isn't coming back." Beth's blue eyes looked as if they had died in her head.

"Yes," Kathryn said sadly, torn between devastation for her mother and vile fury for her father. "And we will have to find somewhere else to live."

"I've lived in this house all my life," her mother went on as a single tear made its way down her pale cheek.

It was the thing which had infuriated Kathryn more than anything. Warren Barton had come into the marriage with very little but his own inflated sense of self-importance. Beth, however, being an only child, had inherited the home she had been born in. It sickened Kathryn that in simply marrying her mother, the property had become her father's.

Furthermore, if what Mr Wolverton had told them was true, and she had no reason to doubt it, there was nothing in law which compelled Warren Barton to provide for his family when he turned on his heel and walked away from them.

Warren had agreed to pay them a small allowance monthly, and given that there was nothing obliging him to do so, it gave it the appearance of charity, almost as if he was doing them some great favour, a favour he had no responsibility to provide. Oh, how she despised him.

"I'm so sorry, Mama. I'm so sorry for the way things are, the unfairness of the world which stacks all the fortune in favour of a man and not his wife. He is a despicable creature."

"Oh, Kathryn, you mustn't," her mother said wearily.

"What are we to do, Mama? The allowance he plans to give us will barely cover rent in the shabbiest of rooms in a shabby part of London. How is that not despicable?"

"It isn't his fault!" Jane said in a vicious snarl.

Kathryn watched as her younger sister's eyes drifted towards their mother, narrowing almost hatefully.

"Then perhaps you might tell me just exactly whose fault it is!" Kathryn said, turning to face her sister, almost regretting her determination never to strike her again.

"He wanted a son, was that too much to ask?" Jane said, parroting words she had heard her father say time and time again. Still, her eyes were on her mother, narrowed and cruel, blaming her for something she could not control.

"You really do show your lack of intelligence sometimes, Jane, not to mention your lack of common sense and your lack of decency. I cannot help but hope that you will one day understand what it feels like to be so cruelly treated by a man as Mama has been so cruelly treated by our father. Perhaps then you will look back on your words and be sorry for them!"

"I hate you!" Jane said, her face reddening as tears rolled down her face. But Kathryn wasn't in a mood to feel sorry for her, to give her leeway for being younger. She had inherited their father's nastiness, and she was certainly not a baby anymore. There was no excuse.

"I think I had rather figured that out for myself," Kathryn said, her tone dismissive as she turned her back on her sister and sat down beside her mother on the couch. Taking Beth's hand, she decided to spend her love and care wisely, only ever on people who deserved it.

Jane stamped out of the room, leaving the door wide open so that her mother and sister might hear her further stamping up every one of the stairs. Well, if she thought that Kathryn or their mother would go running after her, Jane Barton had another shock coming!

"I'm sorry, Kathryn," Beth said and turned miserably to look into her eyes. "If only I had done better. If only I had..."

"No, Mama, you did nothing wrong. You are not to blame for this. There is only one person to blame for this, and I shall despise him until my dying day."

"I'm not strong enough for this, Kathryn. I have never had to make decisions, to make sensible choices, how am I to decide what must be done?

How can I do any of it when all I really want to do is climb back into my bed and curl up in a ball and never, ever come out again?"

"I'm here, Mama. We can make the decisions together. You are not alone." Whilst Kathryn wanted so much to soothe her mother, she wanted even more for her to rail against this life, to roll her sleeves up and do what must be done for her daughters.

However, knowing that her mother couldn't, Kathryn felt *truly* alone, overwhelmed by the enormity of the task ahead of her.

CHAPTER SIXTEEN

*A*rnold Wolverton kept regular contact with Kathryn, ensuring that she was fully informed on the progress of the sale of the family home. She both welcomed and dreaded his visits in equal measure, doing her best to let the ageing solicitor see nothing more than the gratitude. After all, these were things she needed to know.

She had already begun to search for somewhere to live, quickly realising that their options were very limited. Still, at least the allowance her father was providing would allow them to have more than just a single room.

It was a difficult task and being left to her own devices, with no input whatsoever from either her mother or her sister, Kathryn had decided upon a two-room dwelling in Kennington. The rooms were on the ground floor of a larger terraced house on Kennington Road. Whilst the area might not have been the worst, the houses were still fine-looking from the outside, it was clear just how many people lived inside each one. Landlords in the area were managing to squeeze every drop out of every square inch of space. When she had been to look at the rooms, she realised that having only three of them living there was veritable luxury compared to the circumstances of her neighbours.

Mr Richardson, the landlord, was a man who seemed to have been raised in similar circumstances to her own. They seemed to be on a par in terms of class and education, and yet Mr Richardson clearly wanted to display the wealth he had undoubtedly accrued on the backs of the working classes who rented such tiny spaces from him. He wore a very fine suit, with dark grey trousers and a long, tailored jacket to match. His waistcoat was the deepest black, and his shirt the whitest white. He wore a cravat in black rather than a necktie, making himself appear something of an old-fashioned dandy. Kathryn had almost laughed when she looked down at his shoes;

she had never seen a man wearing such shiny patent leather.

"I think you will find my rates are very reasonable given the close proximity to the heart of the city," he said in a braying tone that was designed to make him sound a few rungs further up the ladder of the middle classes than he truly was. In that, he reminded her of her father, an easy comparison which made her dislike Mr Richardson all the more.

"How many people live in this house, Mr Richardson?" Kathryn asked a little sharply, looking around what might well be their new home and wondering how they would survive the claustrophobia.

"It is a very large terrace, Miss Barton," Mr Richardson said waspishly, avoiding a direct answer to her question in the style of a politician.

"Yes," Kathryn said as she stared around the larger of the two rooms.

"I think you will find this provides a very fine kitchen and living space," Mr Richardson went on, and even he sounded unconvinced by his words.

Kathryn followed his pointing finger with her eyes, staring at the space which was to be their kitchen. There was a stove which was, she realised, to provide not only heat for cooking but heat for both rooms. There was a small bench beside it, with a large basin, presumably intended to be used as a sink.

"Where do we get our water?" Kathryn asked doubtfully.

"There is a utility room, you will be pleased to know that your accommodations will be the closest to it. There is a cold water tap and a sink in that room, although you will have to share it with the rest of the house. Still, it will be enough to wash your things and to get water for your daily needs." He let out a sigh. "I'm not really sure where you've come from, my dear, but this really is a good place for the sort of money that you have."

"I'm sure it is, Mr Richardson," Kathryn said, realising that he probably spoke the truth.

Nonetheless, that did not excuse the money that he and his ilk made from people who couldn't afford any better. For the first time in her life, it struck

Kathryn that the less a person had, the less they got for their money. Somehow, it didn't seem fair.

"There is plenty of room in here for you to bring in a dining table and chairs, and a couch if you have one."

"Yes, we shall be bringing our own things." Kathryn closed her eyes for a moment and tried to imagine how her mother's prized chintz-covered couches would look in that cold room which was sorely in need of decoration.

As for their dining table and chairs, it would be foolish to think that they could bring them into so small a space. They would have to make do with the table and chairs from the kitchen of their home in Cleaver Square. That table was small and round and had only four chairs. Still, they were hardly likely to be entertaining the way they had once done, for she could hardly imagine any of her mother and father's friends choosing to visit them on Kennington Road.

"And then, of course, there is the bedroom," Mr Richardson said with a flourish as he strode away from Kathryn and opened the door on the adjacent wall. The door creaked loudly. Its wood looked dry and cracked. Did this man do no maintenance to his properties at all?

Kathryn followed him meekly into the room, dismayed to see how small it was and wondering how they would fit their beds inside it. She realised then that they would have room only for the bed that her mother and father had shared.

Already planning ahead, Kathryn decided that her mother and sister would have to sleep together in that room and Kathryn would have to make do on something temporary in what Mr Richardson had loftily described as the *kitchen and living space*. It would require a little more thought, she knew that, for to sleep night after night on one of her mother's couches would surely ruin it.

"I feel it is my duty to tell you, Miss Barton, that I have several other families interested in these two rooms. I have very few two-room accommodations, and they are becoming more and more popular. Of course, I do have a one-room accommodation on the top floor, which is a little cheaper, if that would suit you better," he said, adding the last with a hint of disapproval. He was looking down on her, and he was enjoying it.

Kathryn added him to the list of people that she hoped would one day experience the very thing they had meted out on others. However, the list was growing day by day, and her energy was dissipating in direct proportion. Despising people certainly did take a lot of effort.

"We will take it, Mr Richardson," Kathryn said and felt desolate. Hearing her words said out loud made it real, made that rotten little space her home. "I shall begin moving our things over for the next few days... if that is acceptable?"

"Perfectly."

"And we shall move in fully in two weeks."

"I will require two months' rent in advance. If and when you choose to leave me, I shall, of course, return the excess rent payment."

"Two months?" Kathryn said incredulously.

"It is to protect myself, Miss Barton. You see, it dissuades people from falling behind on their rent and disappearing in the dead of night to avoid paying it. If a person is two months behind, I evict them immediately and spare myself being out of pocket."

"How very clever of you, Mr Richardson," Kathryn said flatly, handing him back the disapproval he had just handed to her.

"My man will collect the rent from you weekly, and I think it is best to tell you that the wisest thing is to pay on time and to pay every week. I do not know what manner of poor management or disorganisation brings you from your last home to here, but perhaps you might find that things go better for you in the future if you attend to important matters quickly and efficiently."

"I can assure you that it is neither disorganisation nor inefficiency which brings me here, Mr Richardson. But beyond that, sir, it is none of your business." Kathryn glared at him, her bright blue eyes becoming steely, almost daring him to argue back. "And your man," she said with heavy sarcasm, "will not be disappointed when he comes to this door for the rent."

"Well, perhaps you would care to meet me here tomorrow at the same time and you will receive the keys upon payment of the two months' rent in advance."

"I shall be here," Kathryn said, already walking away from him.

She was glad to reach the cool air of a spring morning. She was glad to leave the man who fancied himself a dandy, a fine gentleman in his well-cut suit and his gleaming patent leather shoes. She was glad to turn her back on the judgement and disapproval, the little barbs of humiliation that he had heaped on her one at a time, bit by bit.

Looking back at the house once more, she sighed realising that this was the very best she could have managed with the money they had. With a heavy heart, she turned and walked away down Kennington Road, heading towards her home in Cleaver Square to enjoy its comforts while she still could.

CHAPTER SEVENTEEN

"I'm sorry this all seems to have happened so quickly, Mavis. I just wish there were something else I could do," Kathryn said, having the conversation she had feared most of all.

Mavis Baines was not a woman who had been cut out for service. The truth was that she was too rough and a little lazy, not to mention insolent, but Kathryn's father had wanted the cheapest, and the cheapest was exactly what he got.

"Well, that's it then, ain't it? That's me out on me ear, ain't it?" Mavis said, her grey eyes cold, her lips thin, curled back, like an angry dog.

"I will still pay for these last two weeks; we shan't be leaving straight away." Kathryn felt tearful, guilty, and could hardly manage yet one more emotion to add to the great list of them swirling around inside her. "And I will pay you a further two weeks on top of that, severance pay… if you will."

"Two weeks?" Mavis said, her lip curled back even further.

"I'm afraid it's all I can afford." Kathryn fought back her anger.

Mavis had been fortunate to be employed in any house in London, given that she had come to them without a scrap of experience and no skills whatsoever. It had been Beth who had taught the girl to cook, and Kathryn and Jane who had cleaned and dusted and changed sheets to help out where other households might not.

The truth was that the two weeks' severance pay was something that Kathryn could hardly afford to give and to have it sneered at hurt her deeply.

"You're not the one who's going to be out on the streets, are you?" Mavis said, her voice rich with accusation.

"Mavis, do you imagine that I have very much money to spare? I am moving with my mother and sister into two rooms on Kennington Road. If I had money, real money, do you think I would be doing that?" Kathryn's tone was a little sharp, but she was beginning to feel that Mavis deserved it. "I thought the money might help you whilst you find another position."

Mavis's eyes narrowed, and Kathryn knew why. Mavis was unlikely to secure a position in a household again unless it was at a much lower rate of pay. Even with a good reference, a five-minute interview would be enough for any housekeeper to know that Mavis Baines was not exactly worth her weight in gold.

"Two weeks isn't long to find somewhere, is it? And where am I supposed to live?" Mavis barked as if such questions were Kathryn's responsibility entirely.

Wasn't Kathryn, just fifteen years old, already responsible for *enough* people? Mavis was a young woman of almost twenty, a young woman who, as Kathryn knew for a fact, had family in the area.

"Mavis, can you not stay with your mother?" Kathryn asked and looked at the maid with disbelief; she wasn't going to have the wool pulled over her eyes by this surly servant.

"With her?" Mavis said petulantly. "She's a right old bag!"

"But presumably she won't see you out on the streets!" Kathryn said, beginning to run out of patience. "Particularly if you give her a little of the extra money that I am giving you."

"Why should I give it to her?"

"Well, do as you see fit, Mavis. Really, I am sorry about everything, but my family is suffering too. I'm trying to do my best for you, but I'm also trying to do my best for my mother and sister. There really is only so much *best* to go around!" Kathryn's voice was raised, but it didn't seem to bother Mavis. Mavis simply looked her up and down and clicked her tongue.

"No need to be like that," Mavis added, trying to look hurt but failing miserably. Kathryn began to wonder if the young woman had a single feeling anywhere in her body.

"If you need to go to interviews in these next two weeks, please feel free to do so. I know you're still working here, but I understand that it would give you something of a head start if you were able to start looking now." Kathryn stared at her, seeing no concession, seeing not an ounce of gratitude for a single thing that she was trying to do for her.

"Very well," Mavis said, clearly determined not to say thank you.

"And don't worry about anything other than the kitchen. My sister and I will keep on top of things in the rest of the house for the next two weeks." Why, oh why, was Kathryn bending over backwards to make this awful little woman happy?

"Very well," Mavis said again.

Kathryn began to feel vexed. "Well, I shall leave you to it. I need to return to my mother; she's not feeling at all well today."

"Very well," Mavis repeated, and it was on the tip of Kathryn's tongue to tell the rotten young woman that she could forget all about the extra two weeks' pay. After all, it wasn't as if Kathryn didn't need to hold onto every penny she had.

In the end, however, she simply turned and walked away. In the weeks since her father had walked out on them, Kathryn felt as if she hadn't stopped. Her responsibilities, responsibilities which ought to have been his, were weighing very heavily on her young shoulders, and she didn't have an ounce of strength with which to fight an insolent kitchen maid.

CHAPTER EIGHTEEN

hey were just a mile and a half away from their old home in Cleaver Square, and yet they might have been in another part of the world altogether. Cleaver Square had been out of the way, quiet, no real through traffic. Kennington Road, on the other hand, was a great wide road, a well-used road, perhaps one of the busiest in all of Lambeth.

It was the second night in their new home, the second night in which Kathryn looked set to lay awake until the early hours. She was cold, still struggling to come to terms with the stove in the corner of the room, being almost at war with it constantly since they had arrived. It seemed that every time she opened the little door on the front of the heavy, squat, cast-iron contraption, there were either just a few glowing embers or a cooling pile of ash. Kathryn had adjusted the dampers this way and that, trying to find an optimum setting that would keep the wood-burning but, at the same time, not have it flame away and eat their fuel in a heartbeat. Things had been so much simpler with open fires, and even simpler still with the money to buy as much wood and coal as they could possibly need.

"Are you awake?" Kathryn had been so lost in her own thoughts that her sister's voice in the darkness made her gasp. "Sorry, did I wake you?" Jane went on in a very little voice that reminded Kathryn of her sister as a much younger child.

"No, Jane, I was already awake. What's the matter?" Kathryn sat up on the couch, careful to keep her blankets wrapped tightly around her.

Soon, she would have to find an alternative, not just to keep the couch in good order, but to keep her back in good order also. The couch was comfortable enough to sit on, but she had never imagined for a moment just how uncomfortable it would be to lay down on, to sleep on.

In the end, Kathryn had decided to bring only one of her mother's couches, for the sake of space. She had brought a matching armchair too, thinking that much more practical, but she knew that she would not be able to sleep in that either, certainly not long-term. She heartily wished now that she had brought the mattress from her bed, even if she had been forced to turn it on its side and lean it against the wall during daylight hours. Now, of course, it was lost to her, as was everything else that they had left in the house.

Her father had agreed that most of the furniture would be sold with the house, allowing his wife and daughters to take only the bare minimum. Of course, in the end, even the bare minimum wouldn't fit in their new accommodation, and so the current occupier of their old home in Cleaver Square had been the beneficiary.

"I can't sleep," Jane said again in that tiny voice. "It's so noisy here."

"Sit down next to me," Kathryn said, making room for her sister. In the darkness, she felt Jane settle down by her side.

In the last two days, it seemed to Kathryn that Jane's

anger had been replaced, consumed entirely by her undoubtedly overwhelming fear. She had been quiet, almost silent, and had stopped throwing her mother disapproving looks, leading Kathryn to hope that she had, at least, stopped blaming the poor woman for their current circumstances.

"It really is noisy, isn't it?" Kathryn went on, trying to make light conversation with Jane, hoping to soothe her. "I have been lying here on the couch listening to the clip-clop of hooves all night long. We have only moved a short distance, but it seems we have moved into a part of London where nobody ever goes to sleep." She laughed lightly, but Jane did not. Jane sniffed, and then she sniffed again; a sure sign that she was crying in the darkness.

Kathryn didn't speak, she simply unwrapped herself from her blankets and adjusted them so that they encompassed her sister too. They sat huddled side-by-side on the couch not speaking, listening to the sounds of the busy street beyond. It struck Kathryn that somebody always wanted to be going somewhere, even in the dead of night, and she tried to amuse herself by wondering where exactly they were going. She could hear the rumble of carriage wheels, the clip-clop of hooves, the occasional shout as somebody called into the night for a cab.

Then there were other sounds, much less pleasant. There were other shouts, very different from the hailing of a cab. There were voices raised in anger, although not distinct enough that words could be made out. And then there were the occasional cries, female cries, the sounds of distress.

As the sisters sat there in the darkness listening to this brand-new London, a London they had hardly known before despite living almost on its doorstep, Kathryn could feel her hopes and dreams slipping away from her. With just enough money to survive, how was she to manage nurse training when the time came?

Then she thought of other women, the sort of women who were out in the darkness on that very night, the women whose cries could be occasionally heard. Realising that she had things they did not, Kathryn silently chastised herself. They might not live in such fine surroundings anymore, but they weren't having to go out into the pitiless London streets to earn a living. Of course, she could go about training if her heart was still so set on it. Of course, she could.

"Of course, I can!" she whispered firmly to herself.

"Of course, you can *what?*" Jane asked, her voice wavering.

"Oh, nothing. I'm just thinking out loud, that's all." Kathryn leaned sideways and kissed the top of her sister's head in a moment of uncharacteristic closeness. "Why don't I try to get that evil stove alight again? If we are to be awake, at least we shall be warm." Kathryn tried to laugh, but it was a dull, hollow sound.

CHAPTER NINETEEN

"Where did she say she was going?" Beth asked with an anxious look on her face.

"Just that she was going to walk down to Cleaver Square to see if Carla Renfrew is at home. I suppose she must be, for it seems that Jane has lost track of time," Kathryn said with a light laugh, even though she had something of a sense of foreboding.

Jane had begged to be let out of the house on Kennington Road when it became clear that a little cleaning was in order. Kathryn hadn't minded, knowing that it wouldn't be the end of the world for her to have to clean just two rooms by herself. Of course, had the sheets needed laundering at the same time, she would likely have objected. Still, she was beginning to feel protective of her younger sister once again, keen on the idea of her peace and happiness, and so she had let her go.

"She hasn't seen Carla Renfrew for a long, long time," Beth said, perched on the couch with a heavy shawl wrapped around her shoulders, her pale face peering up at Kathryn as she went about her work. "Not since before your father... your father..." She just couldn't say it. She couldn't give voice to the fact that her husband had left her.

"Then it seems they must have rekindled the friendship," Kathryn said, scrubbing the wooden table which had once rested in a much finer kitchen.

The Renfrew family had lived on Cleaver Square for some years, and Kathryn could only barely remember a time when they hadn't. Carla was a year younger than Jane, but the two had always got along nicely, especially since their families enjoyed very similar circumstances. They were not poor, but they certainly weren't wealthy either. They, too, lived in one of the smaller terraces on Cleaver Square, just as

Kathryn and her family had. Mr Renfrew had a job in the city of a similar status to her father, and so it had been quite natural that the two families had done a little more than just pass the time of day when their paths crossed on the street.

As Kathryn scrubbed, she thought bitterly of how none of the Renfrews had called upon them in the time since Warren Barton had deserted the family. Mrs Renfrew had looked sheepish and embarrassed every time Kathryn had seen her out on the square, her cheeks reddening as she quietly enquired after her mother's health. At the time, Kathryn had been furious, but it was a time when she was furious with just about everybody she met.

However, after some weeks, and entirely unable to sustain such burning fury in her heart for so long, Kathryn had more or less let it go. She realised then that her own family would have behaved in much the same way, likely at the direction of her father. Cleaver Square was a very fine place, but both the Renfrew and Barton families had been squarely on the bottom rung. The families had clung to each other, all the while hoping for bigger and better connections. For one of the families to fail left the other family in something of a quandary. Surely, they couldn't be seen to associate with a fatherless family on Kennington Road and still hope to sow the seeds of friendship with some of the finer families in Cleaver Square. It sickened Kathryn, but she had too much else on her mind to dwell on such associations any longer.

"I hope it's a good day tomorrow, Mama." Kathryn decided to strike up some inconsequential conversation. "If it's a good drying day, I think we should get the sheets washed and some of our clothes."

"Oh," Beth said, staring off into the middle distance and clearly not taking in a single word. Once again, it gave Kathryn the curious feeling of being entirely alone when physically she was not.

"Right, I'm going to the utility room to swill out the mop bucket. I think I'll give the floors another going over." Her mother said nothing at all, and so Kathryn picked up the mop bucket and sauntered out of the room.

By the time Kathryn had finished her chores for the

day, secretly proud of her efforts and enjoying the cleanliness of her surroundings even if she could not enjoy the surroundings themselves, the day was beginning to turn to dusk. She had been so caught up in her work, concentrating only on the task at hand, never letting her mind wander to other things, that she had quite forgotten that Jane was still out. In trying to deny their problems, another one had presented itself while she wasn't looking.

"It's getting late, isn't it?" Kathryn said and looked over at Beth, who hadn't moved an inch from the couch all afternoon. She just sat there, not reading, not sewing, nothing. She just sat and stared into space; it seemed to be her only hobby of late.

"Yes," Beth said vacantly.

"It's getting a little dark," Kathryn went on, hoping that her mother would snap out of it and make the connection.

"Yes," Beth said again.

"And Jane still isn't home, Mama," Kathryn said more firmly, staring at her mother and waiting for some reaction.

"She isn't?" Beth said, looking startled.

"I'd better go and look for her. I'll go down to the Renfrew house and see if she's lost track of time there." Kathryn was already wrapping her cloak around her. It was her good cloak, but she didn't want to be seen on Cleaver Square in the old woollen shawl she wore everywhere else. Perhaps one day she would learn to cope with, even ignore, the humiliation, but that day was not today.

"Should I come with you?" her mother asked, a look of panic on her face.

"No, you stay here in case she returns," Kathryn said with an encouraging smile. Her mother had not set foot outside of the house on Kennington Road since the day they had moved in almost a month earlier. She could hardly be persuaded to move to the window for the smallest amount of fresh air, and Kathryn had come to realise that the idea of the outside world was holding some sort of irrational fear for her mother.

Still, there wasn't time for that now. She had to find Jane.

Kathryn had only taken a few strides along Kennington Road when she was confronted with none other than Jane herself. Jane was puffing and blowing as if she had been running, and Kathryn reflexively seized the girl by her shoulders and stared into her face.

"Jane? Are you all right?" she asked, fearing there was something wrong.

"Yes, I'm all right. Sorry, I didn't realise how late it was."

"You've been at Cleaver Square all this time?" Kathryn asked an uneasy feeling that her sister hadn't been there at all.

"Yes," Jane said.

Kathryn could see her sister's eyes filling with tears even in the falling light.

"Jane?" she said slowly.

"She didn't want me." Her voice broke and Kathryn quickly pulled her to her, giving her a brief embrace.

"Carla turned you away?"

"I didn't even see her. Well, I didn't speak to her. Their maid had me stand on the doorstep, not even inviting me in, and then her mother came out."

"And what did Mrs Renfrew have to say for herself?" Kathryn asked, realising that the fury she had let go of hadn't, in truth, gone very far.

"She said that Carla had gone away for a while, she was staying with relatives. I asked when she'd be back, but Mrs Renfrew said she would be gone for some time. But I didn't believe her, Kathryn." Tears were rolling down her cheeks now.

"Well, perhaps she *did* go to stay with relatives, my sweet." Kathryn didn't believe it either, but a well-timed lie might help to soothe her sister's broken heart.

"No, she didn't."

"But how do you know?"

"Because as I walked away, I turned to look back at their house." Her voice broke again but she forcefully cleared her throat and continued. "I looked up and could see Carla at her bedroom window looking down at me. She looked right at me, but she didn't smile or wave or anything. She just looked sad, and then she turned away from the window and I was left standing there crying."

"I'm so, so sorry, Jane," Kathryn said, taking her sister's hand and leading her back along Kennington Road towards their home. "I'm sure Carla is upset about it too. It seems fully grown men and women are the ones who behave like children, and children are the ones who are forced to behave like adults. It all seems so ridiculous, so petty and pointless, and I wish there were something I could do to change it."

"You don't have to change it, Kathryn. I'm never, ever setting foot on Cleaver Square again as long as I live." Jane spoke with sudden venom. "And if Carla Renfrew were to fall down in the street in front of me, I would walk around her!"

"I understand, really I do." Something then occurred to Kathryn. "But where have you been all this time? It's almost dark, Jane," she went on.

"I just walked around for a while. I went down to the bridge, I stared out at the river for a while."

"You crossed the bridge, didn't you?" Kathryn said,

keeping any hint of accusation out of her tone. "You went looking for him, didn't you?"

"I had this idea that he might have returned to Pirbright and Fullingham."

"And had he?" Kathryn asked, already knowing the answer.

"No, he hadn't. But he must work somewhere, mustn't he? I mean, the sort of work that Papa does, it's better done in the heart of the city, isn't it?"

"I suppose so, but I don't see what difference it makes to us now."

"I'm going to find him, Kathryn," Jane said with firm conviction. She stopped dead in the street right outside the house and refused to move.

"I just..." Kathryn began, but Jane cut her off.

"I'm not going to accept this the way that you have. I'm going to find him and tell him exactly what it's like to live here. I'm sure he cannot know what sort of awful rooms we're living in now. I'm sure if he *did* know, he'd come to his senses. He wouldn't let us live here if he'd seen it with his own eyes. If I can just find him, I can tell him all about it. If I can just find him, this awfulness will be over."

"Jane, he knows how we live."

"How can he know? How can he know when he hasn't seen it?" Jane said, walking again, following Kathryn to the front door of the house.

"Because he knows exactly how much money he allows us every month to live on. I'm sorry, Jane, but he's a grown man of sense, one who has lived and worked in London his entire life. He knows exactly what sort of accommodation can be afforded on the money he gives us. The truth of the matter is that he doesn't care, Jane. If he cared, if he had ever cared, we would not be standing here now having this conversation."

"I just don't believe it." Jane was shaking her head vehemently.

"I know you don't, my dear sister, and I know I cannot make you believe it. But there will come a time when you do, and I shall be here to take you into my arms, that much I can promise you if I can promise you nothing else. Because when it finally hits you, Jane, it will hit you with full force."

"Well, whatever you say, I'm still going to look for him."

"I suppose I can't stop you," Kathryn said, realising that there was nobody left to tell Jane what she could and could not do anymore. With her father gone and her mother absent in all but body, there was no parent for Jane Barton.

CHAPTER TWENTY

Kathryn was almost thankful that Jane was out of the house when Mr Arnold Wolverton called upon them without warning. She hadn't been expecting to see him, given that he ordinarily brought the allowance from her father on the last day of the month. It was only the middle of June, and Mr Wolverton hadn't been due to call upon them for another two weeks.

"Do come in, Mr Wolverton," Kathryn said uncertainly. "I hope all is well?" It was a question, not a statement.

"I'm afraid I do not have good news, Miss Barton." He spoke gravely, his kindly old eyes looking suddenly careworn, even a little ashamed as if he had done something wrong. He cast his eyes in the direction of Kathryn's mother, who was sitting on the couch staring off into the middle distance, wrapped in a blanket, seeming not to have noticed his appearance in their meagre rooms.

"I think that whatever you have to say, Mr Wolverton, must probably be said to me," Kathryn said, knowing that her mother would be of no use whatsoever, whatever it was Mr Wolverton had to say.

"I wanted to warn you of the situation developing. I cannot say for certain, but I cannot deny the possibility that there may be no money for you at the end of this month." He sighed heavily. "Or any other month."

"What is it? What has happened?"

"It appears that your father has moved on again. I daresay he is still somewhere in London, but where, I cannot say."

"Moved on? I don't understand." Kathryn was shaking her head from side to side and wondering if her soul could take another good and firm kick. Probably not.

"I wrote to him on some trifling matter last week, only to have the letter returned to me yesterday morning with a notation that Mr Warren Barton was not known at that address. Fearing some mistake, I made my way across town to the rooms he had been renting and found that he had, indeed, left them."

"My father rented rooms?" Kathryn said, and whilst it was entirely off point, she found it a little curious. She had somehow imagined that he had used the money from the sale of her mother's childhood home to buy another house for himself.

"Yes, some very smart rooms in the centre of the city," Mr Wolverton said as if he had read her mind. He looked annoyed, and Kathryn was certain that Mr Wolverton had no time for a man who could treat himself to fine rooms in the centre of London whilst his wife and daughters had been left to languish in a very different London altogether.

"Could you not find out from his landlord where he had gone to?"

"The landlord either couldn't or wouldn't say," Mr Wolverton said and shook his head solemnly. "And so, I went to his place of work, another firm of stockbrokers of a similar standard to Pirbright and Fullingham, only to discover that he had recently taken employment elsewhere."

"But where?"

"His employer couldn't say," he said and continued to shake his head. "And I really do think that this man, as furious as he was, would have given up any information he had. I think it is fair to say that nobody at Taylor and Scott knows where your father works now."

Kathryn wasn't sure if it was a slip, or if Mr Wolverton had intended to be a little indiscreet. He had dropped the name of her father's most recent employer into the conversation without so much as a raise of his eyebrow. Perhaps it was a mistake, and perhaps it was just the smallest amount of assistance that he could give her. But if nobody at Taylor and Scott knew where her father was, what was the point in her asking them?

"But I suppose that my father might still come to your office with our money. I mean, it's only the middle of the month." Kathryn had a sinking feeling; she was definitely grasping at straws.

"Nobody would be more pleased than me, Miss Barton, if I were proved wrong on this occasion. I am bound to say, however, that whilst I do not know your father terribly well, what I do know of him both sickens and angers me. I cannot help but think that a man who would leave his family without so much as a word to them could very easily walk away from the last vestiges of responsibility he held in their regard. My dear, I think you must plan for it," he said, nodding now instead of shaking his head. "Miss Barton, you must plan for it. You must be very careful with whatever money you have left in your purse, and I think you must find a way to make more. Forgive the intrusion, my dear, but I think it is time for you to seek some sort of employment."

"But what should I do?"

"You are nicely educated, I believe, perhaps you might be able to find some work as a governess. I know it would keep you apart from your mother and sister for much of the week, but at least you would be able to keep a roof over their heads." He paused for a moment and narrowed his eyes as if thinking over what he had just said. "Or at least you would be able to contribute to their roof."

Kathryn didn't know much about the world of governesses, given that the idea of working as one had never entered her head. The very thought of teaching pampered, privileged little children had never appealed to her. Nothing but the thought of her beloved nursing had ever appealed to her. What she *did* know of such work was that it could be very poorly paid, especially for a young woman of her class. She certainly wasn't poor, and yes, she was educated, but she was lower-middle-class at best, and she was sharp enough to know that she would likely end up in a household who would take so much out of her wages for her bed and board that there would likely be very little left at the end of it.

"Thank you for letting me know, Mr Wolverton. You have always been so kind to us, even though you have no responsibility towards us." She felt a little tearful, wondering if this would be the last time she would ever see him. After all, if her father was going to stop the allowance, Mr Wolverton would have no reason to call on them. He somehow represented a link to her old life, to the way things used to be, and the idea of losing him caused an almost disproportionate amount of grief in her heart.

"There is a moral responsibility, Miss Barton. I

cannot make my living out of feckless men like your father and not care an ounce for those they hurt."

Kathryn was beginning to see why it was that Mr Arnold Wolverton worked in such shabby offices in such a lowdown little part of London. It wasn't mismanagement, inability to do his job well, or even some vice like drink or gambling. He just wasn't ruthless enough. He was a good man, a man with morals and values, with far too much decency for the profession he had chosen.

"Thank you, Mr Wolverton. Please know that I am very grateful for everything you have done for us. You must not suffer any guilt over this, I beg you. We would have been absolutely nowhere without your assistance, and if my father chooses to turn his back on us completely now, it is not for your want of trying to have him do the right thing."

"Well, I shall return at the end of the month to let you know one way or the other, Miss Barton, but I could not in all conscience leave it until then. I had to let you know, even at the risk of upsetting you unnecessarily. But I do suggest you make provision of some sort, even if you accept some employment only to reject it if it turns out that I am wrong about your father."

"I will, I promise. You have not led us wrong thus far, Mr Wolverton, and I set a great deal of store in your advice."

"Perhaps, but understand that you are a very strong and resourceful young woman." He cast a brief glance over towards her mother to be sure that she wasn't paying attention. "It has not escaped my notice that you have been forced to shoulder the burden of your family's misfortunes. Nobody should have to do that, most particularly one as young as you." His words were not only kind but absolutely accurate. To hear somebody else give voice to that which she had imagined nobody had noticed, to that which she had suffered alone for so long, brought tears to her eyes.

Mr Wolverton laid a hand on her shoulder, his pale old eyes were kindly and curiously wise. As silly as it was, she wished that he had been her father. He was worth a hundred of Warren Barton, and she was certain that she cared so much more for the strangely cultured old man than she did the man who truly fathered her.

"There now, take this," he said and gave her one of his extraordinarily pristine handkerchiefs. "And this," he went on, and pushed some coins into her hand, firmly closing her fingers around them.

"Mr Wolverton, I couldn't," she said, dabbing at her eyes with his handkerchief.

"Please, Miss Barton, promise me that whenever help comes your way, honest help, you will take it. Your world has become too difficult for you to hold onto such fierce pride." Looking a little emotional himself, he said not another word before turning and quietly leaving their rooms.

With tears rolling down her face, Kathryn opened her hand and stared down at the coins Mr Wolverton had pressed into her palm. Surely, he could not afford to be so generous, for there was enough there that they might survive another month if her father did not, in the end, provide for them.

Drying her eyes completely and stowing Mr Wolverton's pristine handkerchief in the sleeve of her dress, Kathryn decided to say nothing of the money to her mother or her sister. Instead, she would hide it away and keep it safe, and if her father did fulfil his responsibilities and continue to provide their monthly allowance, Kathryn would return the money in its entirety to that kindly old solicitor.

No sooner had she tucked the money away under a loose floorboard than Jane returned, undoubtedly from a day of searching for their father.

"You must be hungry, Jane," Kathryn said, feeling exhausted and knowing that she was putting off the moment when she would have to tell her sister of Mr Wolverton's visit.

"Yes, very hungry," Jane said, looking tired and a little grubby from a day spent wandering the city. Kathryn wished that her sister would give up this foolish occupation, but she had long since come to realise that it was a decision that her sister would have to come to on her own.

"I've got some stew cooking; it will only be an hour or so. Here, I'll cut you some bread and a little cheese whilst you're waiting. It will keep you going." Kathryn smiled at her. It occurred to her that this was the closest the sisters had been in all their lives. Adversity had certainly drawn them together, even if they did not look at that adversity in exactly the same way.

"I think I've tried every stockbroker in London," Jane said, and Kathryn knew she was exaggerating a little.

"Have you tried one called Taylor and Scott?"

"No, I don't think so," Jane said and looked at her hopefully. "Why? Do you know something? Does Papa work for them?"

"He did, apparently. He recently left, so Mr Wolverton tells me."

"When did he tell you?" Jane said a little sharply, assuming her sister had been keeping things from her.

"Just minutes before you arrived home." Jane let out a great puff of air. It was time to tell her sister all about it, although she certainly did not relish the responsibility. "Sit down and eat your bread and cheese, and then I will tell you about it."

CHAPTER TWENTY-ONE

I t was the day that Kathryn let go of her dreams for good. The day she walked through the semi-darkness of the early morning. It was now summer, but she was expected to begin her first shift at six o'clock, and she had to walk for almost an hour to reach the factory in Clerkenwell.

What would this journey be like in the dead of winter? Walking over the bridge and through the dark streets in all weathers. Kathryn could hardly think about it, for this seemed bad enough already.

Just as Mr Wolverton had expected, Warren Barton had finally divested himself of the last of his responsibilities as he saw them. He had not paid, he had not made any contact with Mr Wolverton, and

Kathryn decided there and then to simply assume that he never would. She had searched for employment the very next day, trusting Mr Wolverton and following his advice to the letter.

She had been right to assume that work as a governess would provide little to no help for her mother and sister. It would simply have been a way to keep a roof over her own head, to save herself from certain destitution. It would have left her mother and sister to their own devices. Kathryn knew that they would never, ever manage. Although Jane was thirteen, almost fourteen, like Kathryn, she had never worked a day in her life and, unlike Kathryn, she had never expected she ever would.

As for Beth Barton, she seemed to be sinking deeper and deeper into a silent world, one so far removed from Kathryn's reach that she began to fear that her mother might, sooner or later, end up in an asylum. Certainly, if Jane were left to look after her, something of that nature could quite easily occur. No, there would be no escape to finer surroundings for Kathryn Barton. For Kathryn, there would be nothing but the Warrington match factory in Clerkenwell, the long walk back and forth, meagre pay, and the grinding responsibility of carrying her mother and her sister on her back.

There would be no training in one of the Nightingale's schools, there would be no St Thomas's Hospital for her. There would be no nursing. There would just be this.

Tears rolled down Kathryn's face as she scurried across the bridge. She didn't look back at the hospital; she was heartbroken and desolate enough. She simply concentrated on her surroundings, feeling every whip-stitch of her vulnerability as she hurried along the northern bank of the Thames.

As she headed towards Clerkenwell and the East End beyond, she realised she was in another part of the city which never went to sleep. The tide was out, and mudlarks paraded through the sodden mess that was the riverbank. The children, many much smaller than her, picked through the sludge in the hopes of finding something of value. They barely gave her a second look, being far too intent on their own circumstances to waste time tormenting a young woman on her way to work.

The streets of Clerkenwell were different, however.

There were the remnants of the night before, those who plied their trade at night, getting ready to finish, enjoying a moment or two to jeer and sneer at the young woman hurrying along, the young woman who was somehow so dreadfully out of place.

"Have you got time for a quick one before you go to bed, girl?" A rough-looking man called from the edge of an alleyway between two soot-marred buildings.

Kathryn wasn't so innocent that she didn't understand his meaning, and she wasn't so stupid that she would engage in conversation with the man in any way, even to defend herself from the slur. Instead, she hurried her step, looking determinedly ahead of her, all the while her ears seeking for any sound behind her, in case the man thought to give chase.

By the time she reached the factory, Kathryn was already exhausted. The walk alone was enough to almost finish her, the fear of simply making her way to her place of work taking its toll.

There was already a great throng of women at the door of the factory, steadily becoming an orderly line as they made their way in through the great doors.

Feeling nervous and out of place, Kathryn attached herself to the group, standing at the very back of them.

"Excuse me," she said in a near whisper to a middle-aged woman standing in front of her. "Would Mr Harper be here already?"

"Mr Harper? What's one of your sort want with Mr Harper?" The middle-aged woman said, not whispering as Kathryn had done but booming loud enough for all around to hear. The sharp voice drew attention not only to herself but to Kathryn. She very quickly realised that it had been the woman's intention.

"I spoke to him about a job, a position here."

"A position?" the woman said and started to cackle in a way that was horribly suggestive. "And what sort of *position* is that then?" The women around her began to titter with laughter.

"To work in the match factory, the same as you, I expect," Kathryn said, her cheeks blushing violently. All of London seemed to have a vile edge to it that morning, and she wondered if any job that was open to her now would be any different.

"Jeanette?" The woman turned and bellowed down to somebody at the very front of the line. "Got one for you here. Did Mr Harper tell you to be expecting somebody to train up?"

"Yes, yes," the woman called Jeanette said, sighing as she relinquished her place at the front of the line and made her way over to Kathryn. "I'd better just check it's the right one though," she went on, and there was an edge to her voice that made Kathryn suddenly a little afraid.

Jeanette, a woman in her thirties who was clearly with child, smiled sweetly at Kathryn before reaching out to gently take hold of her chin. Kathryn stood as still as a statue, not knowing what she should do next. What was this? What was happening?

Jeanette then seized her nose with the other hand, and held her chin all the harder, prising her mouth open and seeming to peer inside. Kathryn managed to pull away, and Jeanette was laughing heartily.

"Yes, this is the right one. I've had a look in her mouth and the plum is definitely in there."

"Plum?" Kathryn said, on the verge of tears.

"That's right, Mr Harper told me to expect a plummy-voiced little girl to be coming in this morning," Jeanette went on and grinned at Kathryn. "And I had to check, didn't I?" she went on, her East End accent shrill and grating.

"You couldn't have just asked?" Kathryn said, blinking hard, determined not to cry in front of these creatures, these vultures.

"Don't take on so, girl, we have to make our own entertainment here. You'll get in the swing of it sooner or later!" she said, smiling as if this was some kind of lesson. As if she were doing Kathryn a good turn, a favour, in beginning her tuition immediately.

"So, you will be training me, will you?" Kathryn asked, softening her tone, not wanting to make her life any harder than it was undoubtedly going to be from that moment onward.

"That's right, you'll stick with me for a day or two, and mind you take notice of everything because, by the end of the week, you'll be on your own. You'll be expected to just get on with it then, and woe betide you if you don't, because Mr Harper, well, he ain't no soft touch. He will turf you out on your ear as soon as look at you if you're not pulling your weight, that's all I can tell you."

"Well, I'll bear that in mind," Kathryn said, nodding in what she hoped might appear an appreciative fashion. The truth was, she already hated Jeanette. She hated them all.

It was one thing to be poor, to have to work so very hard, but why was everyone so cruel? They were like sharks scenting blood in the water, anything to amuse themselves. The glee in their eyes was as if hurting somebody else made their own lives seem somehow a little less miserable. They already seemed like a group of women without a shred of humanity, and Kathryn realised that her loneliness looked set to continue in every area of her life.

The factory itself was enormous, almost breathtakingly so. The workforce was largely female, and once inside the building, everybody seemed to know what they were doing. They all set about getting on with things, going about their business, and Kathryn, despite the awfulness of the surroundings, almost looked forward to the day when she could simply become one of them. Knowledgeable, anonymous, just going about her work without anybody's eyes upon her. How her ambitions had diminished!

"It smells awful," Kathryn said, wishing she hadn't spoken the words aloud as Jeanette turned, grinning at her. She had dark brown eyes, narrowed and mocking, and mud-brown hair, which was thin and lank and clinging to her forehead in greasy strings.

"You try copping a lungful of it when you've got the early morning sickness, believe me, that ain't no fun!" Jeanette said.

Kathryn decided to take the opportunity to try to befriend the woman. "How far along are you?" she asked with a smile.

"I'll be squeezing this one out before the end of next month, I reckon."

Kathryn almost winced at the description.

"You must be finding it difficult to work such long days in your condition." It was hard to be sympathetic with somebody who had shown her up so cruelly in front of all the other women, but she was in survival mode.

"It's my feet more than anything, can you believe

that?" Jeanette's face softened, she was clearly not used to somebody caring one way or the other how it was she made her way through each of her long and arduous days.

"It can't help being on them all day, I'm sure." Kathryn was fighting to be understanding. "Are you working right up until the last minute, as it were?"

"Nothing else for it, love," Jeanette said, smiling and shrugging all at once. "I've already got six of these little beggars at home!" she said, patting her stomach and shaking her head. "And an old man who does more spending than saving."

"Yes, men can be very selfish, can't they?" Kathryn said, and felt a moment of solidarity with the woman; she was speaking from her own experience, after all.

"Can't they just!" Jeanette said and smiled more genuinely this time.

If she regretted her treatment of Kathryn outside the factory, Jeanette gave no sign of it. However, in just a few minutes, Kathryn had cleverly found a way to appeal to the woman, and if she could expect no apology, at least she might be spared anymore little humiliations, from Jeanette herself at least. It was a sign of just how far her own standards were slipping that anything less than a full apology would do nicely.

"Come on, then, let's get you started!" Jeanette said, and then took Kathryn's arm to lead her through the factory.

As Kathryn walked, she was aware of being stared at. When she looked casually to the side, she could see that the stare was, in fact, a glare, and the person doing the glaring was none other than Mavis Baines.

Well, as if this life weren't hard enough, now she would be working in the same factory as her old kitchen-maid!

CHAPTER TWENTY-TWO

"*H*ow has she been today?" Kathryn asked as she did every evening when she came back to their rooms from a long day at work and stared sadly at the shell of a woman sitting on the couch.

"Just quiet, the same as always." Jane now spoke with care about their mother, her determination to see their current circumstances as that poor woman's fault seeming to have evaporated.

Jane still searched for their father, and Kathryn had no doubt that she left their mother alone for great swathes of the day as she continued in her occupation. However, Beth seemed none the worse for it. She probably hardly noticed that her youngest daughter was out of the room at all. At least Jane was being kinder to her mother, and Kathryn thought of it as a small victory. She could go about her daily work and not spend her time worrying about what was happening back home.

"That's good, thank you, Jane." Kathryn smiled at her sister.

"I've made some stew," Jane said with a little flash of pride. "It's not up to much, and there's only a very small bit of meat in it, but I think it's quite tasty."

"Oh, that is wonderful," Kathryn said, relieved that she wouldn't have to begin working on something for the three of them to eat after so many hours breathing in the dreadful phosphorus at the match factory. "I really am very grateful."

"It's the least I can do." Jane stirred the stew just as the candle on the kitchen table guttered and went out.

Jane huffed under her breath, and whilst the rooms hadn't been plunged into complete darkness, there certainly wasn't enough light to cook by. There were two candles on a shelf on the other side of the room, but they really only shed light on their mother who, as always, was perched on the couch staring into space.

"Oh! You're glowing!" Jane said, her voice full of wonder as she stared through the semidarkness at her sister. "Well, not you, but your dress!"

Kathryn looked down and could see that her dress did seem to shine just a little. When Jeanette had first told her about the glow of phosphorus, Kathryn had wondered if she was simply being teased. Well, apparently not.

"Oh, so I am," Kathryn said and laughed, vaguely amused. "One of the women said that this might happen. I've been working in the part of the factory which makes the lucifers."

"The matches that don't need a box?" Jane said.

"The very same. The ones that you can strike on anything."

"Well, I don't suppose you have one about your person now, do you?" Jane said, and Kathryn laughed all the harder.

"Sorry, not a single one."

Jane searched the top of the bench next to the stove, quickly locating a box of matches and striking one, relighting the candle on the kitchen table. As the room lit up, the phosphorescent glow from Kathryn's clothing magically disappeared.

"What's so different about the lucifers? I mean, I know you can strike them on anything, and you don't need the box, but why do they make you glow?"

"They're made from something a little different. They call it yellow phosphorus. The smell is truly awful," Kathryn said and sighed as she settled herself down at the kitchen table and stared at the candle's flame. "It's a sort of awful mustard coloured gloop."

"Gloop?" Jane said and giggled. "What do you mean?"

"It's sticky awful stuff, it has the consistency of an egg-custard or something like that. It's in great vats, and we have to roll the wooden matchsticks in it. It dries then, creating that little nub on the end of the match, the bit you strike."

"So, it's the yellow... what did you call it?"

"Phosphorus."

"So, it's the yellow phosphorus that makes you glow?"

"Amongst other things, yes," Kathryn said but decided not to continue with explanations. Life was hard enough for all of them, including Jane, and Kathryn had decided that her little sister did not need to know of the more distressing effects that yellow phosphorus might have.

"I think this might need a little more salt," Jane said, tasting a spoonful of her stew and smacking her lips in a dainty sort of way, almost like a fine chef in a fine restaurant.

Kathryn was relieved that her sister had turned her attention to other things and that they could leave their conversation of the match factory right there.

The truth was that Kathryn wished that she didn't know what the yellow phosphorus could do. She understood entirely why Mr Harper had chosen not to tell her of any of the pitfalls of working in a match factory when she first approached him for employment. He was a sour sort of a man, and she hardly imagined that he cared a jot for the women who succumbed to the worst ravages of the yellow phosphorus. The same way that the people who *had* to have lucifers, who simply couldn't manage to carry their matches in a box, likely wouldn't care either that such a convenience to them came at a great price to others.

Kathryn had heard little mutterings of strike action amongst the women, and whilst she admired such courage, she privately hoped that it wouldn't come to fruition, at least not yet. She had only just begun to find her feet, and whilst her earnings were so little, given the work that she did and the hours she spent doing it, at least it was enough to keep them going. By keep them going, of course, it kept the roof over their heads and meant that they might have an inch or two of meat in their stew once a week. It was hardly living, but for now, *existing* would have to suffice.

Content to watch her sister stirring the stew and adding a little extra salt, Kathryn thought of some of the awful things she had seen in the week she had worked at Warrington's match factory. She had quickly learned that when she worked on the lucifers, she shouldn't eat or drink a single thing for the entire day. She generally ate the bread she packed herself for her midday meal when she was still walking to work in the morning, filling her belly and hoping that she could make it to the end of the day without stomach pains and feelings of faintness.

She had not only seen but had experienced for herself, the dangers of eating or drinking whilst working on the lucifers. Just the tiniest amount of yellow phosphorus ingested could make a person terribly sick, and in the darkness, as the women filed out of the factory every night, the evidence of small and curiously glowing piles of vomit stood out like ridiculous steppingstones away from their day's work.

It had only happened to Kathryn once, but she was determined that it would never happen again. She knew that to ingest that evil stuff could result in symptoms far worse than a little vomiting.

On only her second day, Kathryn had found herself drawn to look at a woman who seemed to be working in a space all by herself. She was doing the same job that everybody else was doing, as far as Kathryn could see, and yet she seemed to be strangely ostracised.

"Why does that woman work by herself?" Kathryn asked Jeanette, unable to stem the tide of her curiosity.

"Because she stinks."

"I know I've only been here a couple of days, but I can tell you very definitely that she isn't the only one," Kathryn said.

Jeanette had laughed. "You're sort of funny really, aren't you? Not as bad as I thought in the beginning."

High praise indeed.

"Surely, she doesn't smell so badly that she has to be left all on her own," Kathryn had persisted.

"She's got the Phossy jaw, love. Every time she opens her mouth, the smell's enough to knock you off your feet. Close-up, is just too much for everybody else. She is not the first, and she won't be the last. All you have to do is hope it never happens to you, the way I hope it never happens to me."

After a little more effort and persistence, Kathryn managed to extract a few details from Jeanette. Phossy jaw, a colloquialism used to describe a condition known as phosphorus necrosis of the jaw, was something much feared by the women who worked at Warrington's match factory. It was feared by the men, too, most of whom had very little to do with the production of the lucifers.

Mr Harper involved himself very rarely, hovering some distance away from the great vats of yellow phosphorus, barking orders and chastisement at the women from afar rather than face-to-face. What cowards these men were! Sending the women into danger day after day and yet assuming themselves to be bigger, better, and stronger by dint of the fact that they had been born male and not female. It was a sort of hypocrisy which reminded her, curiously, of her own father.

To discover the effects of phosphorus necrosis of the jaw had been truly horrific to Kathryn, so much so that she hadn't been able to find the words to talk to Jane about it, or indeed anybody who didn't work within the four walls of the match factory. It was simply too distressing and she knew she couldn't tell her younger sister how a little phosphorus could work its way into the jaw through the smallest hole in a person's teeth, and then work its evil magic to destroy the bone, pushing out tiny pieces until the jaw receded so badly that the sufferer was rendered almost chinless.

The sight and smell of such women made them pariahs, and yet curiously didn't seem to make them unemployable. However, whilst the condition itself was far from uncommon, the sight of such women in the workplace was. As Jeanette explained it to her, at the first sign of symptoms, a woman was expected to have each and every one of her teeth extracted immediately to slow or stem the progress of the awful disease. The first signs were, apparently, a toothache, and Jeanette had told her in a strange and unaffected tone of a woman who had been thrown out of Warrington's for refusing to have her teeth removed when old Mr Warrington had demanded it.

"Kathryn? You look unwell," Jane said, staring at her with concern, the spoon she had been using to stir the stew still in her hand.

"Oh, no, I'm just tired," Kathryn said, glad to have been sharply drawn out of her fears.

Fears of a simple toothache could now be added to the great list of things that she had to be afraid of. The fear of being treated like a leper for the crime of simply doing an awful job for awful pay. And now, ideas of a slowly rotting lower jaw were enough to make her wonder if she could manage a single spoonful of the stew her little sister had so kindly prepared.

CHAPTER TWENTY-THREE

"*J*ane, please do not lie to me, I know you haven't been to church this morning." Kathryn was tired and angry. She had but one day off every week, and she could well do to spend it resting, not arguing with a belligerent younger sister.

"Girls, please," Beth Barton said weakly from her usual perch on the couch.

"I'm sorry, Mama, but one of us has to worry about Jane, don't we?" Kathryn said, and felt a dreadful stab of guilt as she saw a single tear track a course down her mother's soft, pretty face. "Oh, Mama," Kathryn said, leaving Jane sitting at the kitchen table with her arms folded guardedly across her chest as she sat down on the couch to comfort Beth. "We're not arguing, we're just having a conversation. I am just trying to keep Jane safe, that is all."

"I wonder when Warren will be coming back. He was always better at these things than I am."

"Mama, I do wish you would understand that he isn't coming back. I have told you time and time again that he left us, that he doesn't even provide us with a little money anymore. He has cut all ties with us, and we have to find a way to make this life work without him." Kathryn hated to be the one to do it, but somebody needed to drag their mother out of her dreamworld.

Fearing more and more that Beth might one day end up in the asylum, Kathryn had tried everything to have her mother face the truth. Beth had never been strong, but the woman she had once been would certainly be more helpful to Kathryn now than the woman she had become.

"He's probably busy at the new house, my dear. As soon as he has it ready, he'll be coming for us." Not even looking at Kathryn, Beth smiled.

Kathryn kissed her mother's cheek and got up from

the couch, unable to hear any more of her mother's delusions.

"I will find him, Mama, never you fear," Jane said from across the room, but Beth had already retreated into her silent world and didn't seem to hear her.

"Oh, Jane, it is hard enough that Mama refuses to look at the world as it is, without you joining her. He isn't coming back, not even if you find him. Your time would be better spent on other things. Your education, perhaps."

"My education?" Jane said and laughed a little viciously. "Do you really think your work at the match factory is going to pay for a tutor?"

"That's not what I meant. There are books, Jane, things that you can do to teach yourself."

"And where are these books, pray tell?" Jane said sarcastically, a very firm nod to her old way of doing things back in their fine home in Cleaver Square.

"There is a public library in Kennington, Jane. You could go there to do your learning. You can make your prospects so much better."

"Like yours?" Jane shook her head. "Forgive me for

not wanting to study myself into short-sightedness only so that I too, when the time comes, can stride out of the match factory in the evening glowing like a candle."

"I think you are already short-sighted," Kathryn said waspishly. Her anger was bubbling, and worse still, she knew that her anger was justified. "For if you weren't, you would be able to see that I am working at the match factory so that you don't have to. You have the time to improve your circumstances, and when you have educated yourself to a certain level, I will support you through whatever training you need to do to have a better kind of employment than I do."

"There is no need to martyr yourself for me, Kathryn," Jane said, without a hint of gratitude for all that her sister was prepared to give up.

For a moment, Kathryn closed her eyes and imagined running away. She imagined taking that once thought of position of governess, living safely under somebody else's roof, poorly paid, ignored, but safe. With no responsibility save for teaching an insolent child to read and write. No fear of the toothache, the little swelling that would herald the beginning of the end for her beautiful face. Perhaps even her life.

"Nothing changes with you, does it?" Kathryn said, feeling her insides begin to quiver as she fought hard to keep a lid on her anger for her sister.

"Nothing changes with you either, does it? And no, I didn't go to church this morning. Why should I? We haven't been to church since..."

"Since our father *abandoned* us?" Kathryn said, feeling a little thrill of pleasure as she saw her sister's face fall. Well, Jane had been spiteful, and it didn't hurt to have her reminded of her own pain once in a while.

"Well, you don't want to go either! You don't want to sit there and be judged by the people who used to be our friends, our neighbours and acquaintances, do you?"

"No, I freely admit that I do not. But then I'm not lying about it, am I?"

"I'm only lying because you don't want to hear the truth."

"And that truth is, Jane?"

"That I am getting somewhere. I am very close to

finding Papa, and when I do, I shall be sure to tell him that you had no faith in him whatsoever."

"Don't bother to tell him; if you *do* find him, I will be sure to tell him myself." Kathryn was snarling. Where had that closeness gone? Why did their father always come between them? Even when he was nowhere to be found, he managed to dig that great furrow which kept the sisters apart.

"You don't think I'll find him, do you?"

"I'm certain of it."

"Well, after today, I think you might be eating those words." Jane looked suddenly self-satisfied.

"Oh?" In spite of herself, Kathryn felt a little jolt of hope. Even though she knew the truth of it, there was still a child inside her which hoped and prayed that her father would save her.

"I met with a man this morning from Taylor and Scott... if you must know. He hasn't been able to speak to me at his office, because his employer wouldn't be at all happy about it. But he knows that I'm looking for our father, and he told me this very day that he intends to help me."

"If he doesn't know where our father is, how on earth can he help?"

"Because he knows the stockbroker business. He knows so many people in that business that he can put the feelers out."

"Feelers?" Kathryn said incredulously, but there it was again, that little spark of hope.

"He can ask questions; he can help me to track him down. You needn't look like that, Kathryn. I think it is terribly kind of him to go out of his way, and if you don't, then that is your shame and not mine."

"I'm sure he will be very helpful to you, Jane. Perhaps he might even be able to help you find our father. The only problem is, my dear, that when he finds him, will he be able to convince that dreadful man to take the responsibilities that are his? You are heading for a fall, sister, and I am starting to think that it is the only thing which will bring you to your senses."

"Oh, mind your own business!" Jane said, and got up from the table, putting a light shawl around her shoulders.

"Where are you going now?"

"Out!"

"There are things to do in this house, Jane!"

"It is not a house; it is just two horrible little rooms."

"Two horrible little rooms that still need cleaning. You promised to help me."

"It won't take you long." Jane was being dismissive, and Kathryn felt like crying. She had worked her fingers to the bone all week, risking so much more than Jane was aware of, and this was how she was to be treated.

"I have been working for the last six days without a break, Jane. The very least you can do is help me so that I may take a little rest before I have to begin it all again."

"And what about me? Left here looking after our mother." Jane clicked her tongue as if to stay at home was the worst sentence that could have been passed upon her. "Cooking every day and making sure that you have something to eat. When do I get a rest?"

"Perhaps you would feel a little more rested if you

stopped looking for a man who didn't want to be found."

"That's it, I'm going," Jane said, turning her back and flouncing out of the door, clearly having no sensible argument to offer.

Kathryn crossed the room and looked out of the window, watching her sister marching away down Kennington Road with the air of one who has been greatly wronged. She then turned to look back at her mother who seemed to have missed almost the entirety of their argument, contenting herself to live in her dream world, the world in which her husband was simply making their new house spick-and-span before coming to rescue them.

Feeling that she didn't have an ounce of energy left with which to clean their little rooms, Kathryn sat down at the kitchen table and cried for all she was worth.

CHAPTER TWENTY-FOUR

*T*he chatter seemed to be heightened somehow when Kathryn joined the throng of women standing outside Warrington's match factory in the pale early morning light. She hovered somewhere near the back of them, searching for any sign of Jeanette.

In the few short weeks since Jeanette had trained her in the art of making matches, the two had developed a curious sort of friendship. Jeanette still teased her, but it was clear that she didn't despise her as she had done in the beginning. And Kathryn, for her part, had done her best to forget that first day, along with some of Jeanette's coarser, more cutting comments. Still, she realised that Jeanette meant more to her than simply being symbolic of the best of a bad bunch. She actually *did* care for her.

"I thought she was looking like she was ready to drop yesterday," one woman was saying to another within Kathryn's earshot. "And she always worked up to the last minute with the rest of them."

"Excuse me, are you talking about Jeanette?" Kathryn asked, trying to be friendly and bold all at once.

"Yes, haven't you heard?" The woman looked at her, and there was something strange in her countenance. She looked sad and gleeful all at once. Kathryn felt a dull heaviness in the pit of her stomach.

"Heard what? Has Jeanette had her baby?"

"That she has, girl," the woman said, her eyes wide. Surely, childbirth was commonplace, not something to be overly excited about in a workplace filled with women.

"She'll be off work for a little while yet then?" Kathryn said, trying to keep the conversation going.

"She'll be off work a little longer than that," the woman went on, barking a short, mirthless laugh.

"Why? What happened?" Kathryn asked, her heart beginning to pound.

"What happens to enough of us, that's what!" the woman said, glaring at her as if that were explanation enough.

"What?" Kathryn said and surprised both women with her sudden firmness. "Why don't you just tell me!"

"All right, all right, keep your hair on!" One woman said while the other shook her head in annoyance. "She died, that's what. Not everybody comes through it, do they?"

"Is that the truth? Are you really telling me that Jeanette died in childbirth?"

"Not two hours after leaving here last night, by all accounts."

"Oh, no." Tears sprang to her eyes. "Poor Jeanette."

"Now don't you go starting that, girl or Mr Harper will see you. Save your tears for when you get home, they won't do you no good in a place like this, you mark my words." As harsh as those words were, they were delivered with a strange sort of compassion.

"That's right, you pull yourself together until the time comes for you to fall apart. Well, here we go, girls!" the woman said a little more loudly. "Another day at the workhouse!"

With that, the women stopped their chatter and began to make their way into the match factory. Seeing Mr Harper in the doorway marking off the names as the women filed past him, Kathryn took the harsh but sensible advice. She gritted her teeth and concentrated on thinking of absolutely nothing. She already knew enough of Mr Harper's ways to know that he would have little sympathy with one of his workers dissolving into floods of tears.

Kathryn did an admirable job of keeping going that day, fighting her feelings, fighting all thoughts of Jeanette.

"Right, Kathryn, you've got the rest of the afternoon working on the lucifers," Mr Harper said, seeming to appear out of thin air.

"Yes, Mr Harper," Kathryn said and felt so low that she didn't suffer the ordinary stab of fear that she felt when being moved from the red phosphorus matches to the yellow phosphorus ones. She understood now that the red phosphorus matches were more expensive to produce and did not have the same qualities that made the lucifers such a convenience.

"Well, don't just stand there, get on with it. You've been moping about all day, I've seen you, and let me tell you, you're not paid to mope about. You're paid to work, my girl, and work you will do, or you'll find yourself out on your ear."

"Yes, Mr Harper," Kathryn said, fighting an urge to tell the rotten little man to *stick his job where the sun didn't shine.* She smiled to herself; the indelicate phrase was something she had heard Jeanette say time and time again.

Kathryn made short work of setting herself up at a bench in the lucifer room. It seemed strange not to be going there with Jeanette, to have that woman's constant complaints and chatter filling her ears.

"Oh, look who it ain't!" came a voice she recognised. She looked up to see Mavis Baines glaring at her.

In the weeks that Kathryn had worked at Warrington's, Mavis hadn't spoken a word to her. She hadn't been friendly, that was for certain, but she had kept her thoughts to herself. Or at least she hadn't spoken them aloud to Kathryn. When a little titter of amusement came from the women working around Mavis, Kathryn quickly gathered that she must surely have been a topic of conversation more than once amongst the little group.

"Hello, Mavis," Kathryn said, giving her a brief smile and hoping that would be enough to placate her.

"Hello, Mavis," Mavis said in an exaggerated version of Kathryn's more cultured accent.

Kathryn said nothing.

The other women laughed, and Kathryn suffered that awful, sweeping sense of loneliness.

"Not so full of yourself now that your protector has up and died, are you?" Mavis went on, clearly determined not to simply leave her alone.

"Mavis, I don't think there is anything to laugh about, do you? A woman has died in childbirth and you are making as much out of it as you possibly can! Can you not see how despicable that is?" Kathryn said, unable to bite her tongue.

The truth was that Jeanette really had been a sort of protector, she could see that now. Despite their shaky start, despite the fact that Kathryn had never truly forgiven Jeanette for the day when she had publicly opened her mouth in search of an imaginary plum, still, she had looked after her in the weeks that had followed.

"What did I tell you, girls? Miss hoity-toity here still thinks she can tell me what to do. Well, hear this, Miss hoity-toity; I ain't your kitchen maid no more, am I?" As rough as Mavis had always seemed within the four walls of their fine little terrace in Cleaver Square, she seemed rougher than ever now. Her accent was more East End than it had ever been, and Kathryn wondered if she hadn't exaggerated it further still as a means of fitting in with the other women, making herself one of them.

"Just leave me alone, Mavis." Kathryn carried on with her work, determined to ignore the hateful little creature.

"I do as I please now, you don't get to tell me what to do."

"No, but I'm sure that Mr Harper does."

"Oh, running off to tell teacher, are you?"

JESSICA WEIR

"Without a moment's hesitation, Mavis. Why on earth should I care what you think about me?"

"It's not just what I think about you," Mavis said, her cold grey eyes narrowed with amusement. "Don't you worry, I've told the girls how your old dad up and left you all, you pampered little madams all holed-up in two rotten little rooms on Kennington Road!"

"My life is none of your business." Kathryn felt sick; this day was already one of the worst, and now she was left wondering exactly how it was that Mavis knew so much of her personal circumstances.

She had never discussed with her the fact that Warren Barton had deserted his family, even though it was perfectly obvious that he had. But quite how Mavis knew that Kathryn now lived with her mother and sister in two rooms on Kennington Road was beyond her. Of course, she still wasn't a part of that world. Gossip undoubtedly flowed from one mouth to another amongst the working classes just as easily as it did amongst the middle classes. Either way, it seemed that Mavis, with Jeanette no longer there to provide a buffer, was going to make the very most out of taunting and belittling her.

"We'll see about that." Mavis was full of bravado, showing off to the women all around her.

"You're right, Mavis, we *will* see about that," Kathryn said, sounding bold as she issued her thinly veiled threat, all the while feeling anything but brave.

It seemed to do the trick for a little while at least, for Mavis turned her attention back to her work, and Kathryn found herself in the slightly more enviable position of being entirely ignored. To be ignored was certainly preferable to being perpetually tormented.

The day had seemed twice the length of any other day she had worked before, and Kathryn knew that it was her longing to be out of there so that she might give vent to the emotions swirling inside her that seemed to be stopping time. It was as if she was to be denied a good cry, just to add to everything else that she had been denied in life of late. However, the laws of time and space reasserted themselves once more, and the end of the day finally did come.

"See you tomorrow, Miss hoity-toity!" Mavis bellowed loudly over the throng of chattering women leaving the factory that evening. It caused others to turn and look, and Kathryn could hear much sniggering amongst the crowd. Did they all hate her?

She hung back, knowing that her tears were not far away and determined that not one of those awful women would see them. When they had finally dwindled away, leaving her standing outside the factory all alone, Kathryn gave in. She let her tears flow, unchecked at first before she pulled a handkerchief from the sleeve of her dress and pressed it over her face.

The handkerchief was monogrammed, *A.W*, the handkerchief that Mr Arnold Wolverton had given her so many weeks ago when he had sadly informed her that her father had once again disappeared. Staring at the lettering, her tears became sobs.

"It's hard to ignore them, isn't it? But try not to let them get to you so terribly." She assumed the male voice behind her came from Mr Harper, and she quickly turned around.

"I'm sorry, Mr Harper, I..." She trailed off; it wasn't Mr Harper.

"No, not Mr Harper," he said and laughed. He was a young man, and there was something strangely familiar about him, although she couldn't place him. Being too distressed to think straight, Kathryn simply stood there looking at him, wondering who on earth he was.

"Forgive me, my name is Mitchell."

"Oh, I see," Kathryn said, drying her eyes as best she could and trying to get a fix on the young man's face in the fading light outside the factory. "Do you work at the factory, Mr Mitchell?"

"Yes, but it's not *Mr* Mitchell, just Mitchell. Mitchell Warrington."

"Mitchell Warrington?" she said and felt a little fearful.

"Yes."

"You must be related to Mr Warrington, sir." She had only seen the great Mr Warrington from afar, and he was a far cry from this young man. He was older, of course, and looked perpetually disgruntled, angry even. This young man had an open, pleasant face.

"Yes, John Warrington is my father," he said and seemed somehow disappointed by the whole thing.

For a moment, Kathryn forgot all that was hurting her and almost laughed.

"I haven't seen you on the factory floor before, Mr Warrington." Kathryn was searching about for something to say.

"Ah, but you will do in the future. I have just returned to London from Oxford."

"I see, Mr Warrington," Kathryn said, wanting to ask more but realising that her place was very different these days in conversations. With such a reduced status, she did not dare risk any hint of impertinence.

"Please, just Mitchell. Mr Warrington is my father, and I should like to be better regarded than he is by the people who work here," he said and laughed. "So, what's your name?"

"Kathryn Barton," Kathryn said simply, looking up into what she realised was a very handsome face indeed, and still familiar to her. Nonetheless, she was certain that they had never met. Surely, she would know the son of her employer if they had ever been introduced before.

He was tall, a good deal taller than Kathryn, and he

had hair that could equally be described as either a light brown or a dark blond. In the fading light, she couldn't tell the colour of his eyes, but they looked kindly nestled as they were in so fine a face. He was older than her, perhaps twenty to twenty-two, but certainly no older than that.

"Well, Kathryn, don't let the other women get you down. I know it's hard, and I know it's easy for me to say, but they really aren't worth your tears."

"Well, one of them was," she said sadly. "Jeanette Smith."

"Oh, the woman who died?" he said, a look of genuine regret on his face. Kathryn felt her eyes fill with tears again, but this time because she realised that he was the first person who had spoken that day of Jeanette with any real kindness.

"Yes."

"It is a terrible tragedy for a woman to die that way, especially when she leaves behind other little ones." He surprised her, seeming to have real knowledge of Jeanette's background. Yet there had been nothing about Mr Harper, or any of the others who worked in the upper echelons of Warrington's matches, which gave the vaguest indication that they even cared, never mind that they knew of the children that Jeanette had left behind.

"I can hardly think of it. I have waited all day to step foot outside and shed my tears for her."

"Then it must have been a very difficult day for you, Kathryn, to have tried to hold so much inside."

"It really was. Thank you, Mr Warrington."

"Mitchell!" he said and gave her a cheeky sort of grin.

"Mitchell," she said and laughed. "Well, I suppose I ought to make my way home."

"You be careful on the bridge," he said cryptically.

"How do you know I cross the bridge to go home?"

"Just you be careful," he went on and chuckled. "No stopping suddenly to look up at St Thomas's Hospital! The next man you collide with might be bigger than me and knock you over." And with that, he disappeared back inside the factory.

"Oh!" Kathryn said out loud to herself. "Oh!" she said again. She realised immediately where she recognised him from. He had been the young man she had bumped into on Westminster Bridge so, so long ago. Back when her life had been something else altogether and she still had dreams of being a nurse, of working inside that wonderful building.

It was a bittersweet moment. She felt suddenly like she had a friend, an ally, and yet his very existence reminded her so sharply that her world had changed for the worse and would never, ever be the same again.

As she set off for home, her tears returned.

CHAPTER TWENTY-FIVE

*I*t was two days before Kathryn actually saw Mitchell Warrington on the factory floor. There were offices on the far west corner of the great factory building, and although she had never been inside any of them, she knew that there were many.

For the most part, men worked in the offices, safely tucked away, shielded from the worst effects of the evil yellow phosphorus. There were buyers, salesmen, accountants, and clerical officers. One or two women were employed in the offices, but Kathryn didn't know what they did.

On the factory floor, only maintenance men and Mr Harper could usually be seen, so when Mitchell

Warrington strode out for the first time, one hundred pairs of eyes swivelled in his direction.

"That's old Mr Warrington's boy, so they say," one of the women working close by Kathryn on the lucifers said excitedly.

"Put your tongue back in your head, you dirty old bag!" Mavis said crudely, and all the women laughed, including the one who had just been insulted. "You're old enough to be his mother!"

"Grandmother, more like!" another said, following Mavis' lead. Still, the woman didn't appear insulted, and Kathryn realised it was just the way they all were. They spoke harshly and expected to be spoken to in the same way. It was all so awful; all so without hope in her eyes.

"Best leave young bucks like him to us young women who know what to do with him!" Mavis went on, Kathryn couldn't help but wince.

Mavis glared at her, and Kathryn turned her head away, silently continuing with her work. However, she could feel Mavis' eyes on her and knew that this wasn't over yet.

"Well, look at Miss hoity-toity! Her little cheeks all flushed. She must know what we're talking about, girls, mustn't she?" Mavis said, to a raft of mumbling approval from her clutch of devotees. "Maybe she's even had a look at him herself and fancies a go, what do you all reckon?"

"Don't reckon she'd know what to do with him, Maeve!" said one of Mavis's rougher friends. "And I don't reckon he'd want her if she did!" she went on, and Mavis and her cohort roared with laughter.

Feeling utterly miserable, Kathryn kept her head down. She wasn't about to argue her case, not with such hopelessly stupid women. The only point that would serve would be to fuel the fire, giving them more to work with, more to torment her with. They could carry on all they wished, but they would carry on without her input.

"Hush, he's coming over!" Mavis said, instantly silencing the women around her.

Keeping her eyes on her work, Kathryn didn't know exactly who was coming over. It could be Mr Harper, for all she knew, and she was determined not to look up. She was already blushing from the low conversation, and she couldn't bear Mavis to see her scarlet cheeks.

"Everything all right, ladies?"

"Yes, Mr Warrington," Mavis and her friends chimed as one. They sounded suddenly sweet, innocent almost, and recognising the voice of Mitchell Warrington, Kathryn knew why. They were all trying to appeal to him.

"Kathryn?" he said, and she looked up, feeling Mavis's eyes boring into her. "How are you?"

"I'm well, thank you, Mr Warrington," she said, willing him not to repeat that she was free to call him Mitchell.

"Jolly good." He nodded, and Kathryn could almost feel Mavis' hatred rolling off her in waves, making its way across the great workbenches right into Kathryn's heart. "Well, sorry to drag you away, but you're needed down the other end."

By *down the other end*, he meant that she was to come away from the yellow phosphorus, the lucifer tables, and make her way to the other end of the factory to work on the ordinary red phosphorus matches.

"Yes, Mr Warrington," Kathryn said, and quickly tidied up her workstation before turning to follow him.

"Yes, Mr Warrington," she heard Mavis whisper in a ridiculous parody.

"That Mavis really is something else, isn't she?" he said as the two walked side-by-side along the outer edge of the factory floor.

"She despises me," Kathryn said and laughed. "And I'm already used to it."

"You shouldn't have to get used to behaviour like that." He turned to look at her as they walked, and she realised that, had she seen him in full light outside of the factory that evening, she would have recognised him immediately as the man she had almost knocked over on Westminster Bridge.

He was a fine man, somehow more cultured than his father appeared to be, well-spoken, and likely well educated. He was not only handsome, but he had a nice face, faded pale green eyes that were open, honest, and kind. She was glad that her cheeks had already been flushed by the time he had reached her, for he would certainly have noticed them blushing now.

"Perhaps Mavis has her reasons," Kathryn said a little cryptically.

"And what in the world might they be?" he said, grinning, looking as if he didn't believe there could be a reason in all the world to dislike Kathryn Barton.

"She used to work as a housemaid for my family."

"I can't imagine that you treated her terribly." His eyebrows were raised, and it was clear that he wanted to know a little more. After all, she had handed him a very small and very tantalising piece of information about herself. Here she was, one of the match girls, claiming to have once been possessed of a kitchen maid. Even Kathryn had to admit that it was the sort of titbit which begged to be questioned further.

"No, far from it. And she wasn't a very good maid either. The problem was, Mavis wanted to work as a maid without actually having to work as a maid... if that makes sense."

"You mean she was as lazy then as she is now?" he said, putting the thing much more practically.

"Yes, I suppose that is what I mean. Although, now you'll think me no better than the rest of them, being just as nasty as they are."

"Without knowing you, I already know that there isn't a nasty bone in your body."

"And just how would you know that, Mr Warrington?"

"Mitchell."

"That is very kind, Mitchell, but for my own sake, I think, perhaps, it ought to just be *Mr Warrington* on the factory floor," she said in a whisper. "Although, thank you kindly for deciding I don't have a nasty bone in my body. There, I have at least one ally in this building."

"And now I have at least one ally in this building," Mitchell said, offering an equally tantalising titbit.

Now, they both wanted to know a little more about

each other. But of course, now was not the time to explore it. There was work to be done, and there were women the length and breadth of the factory casting glances in their direction.

"So, you said that I needed to work on the red phosphorus?"

"I'll find you a space," he said and winked at her.

"But I thought..."

"I just wanted to give you a little break from those awful women for a while." He shrugged his shoulders and chuckled. "Or at least take you away from one set of awful women and hand you to another."

"They're not all as bad as Mavis, believe me. At least the ones in this section will simply ignore me."

"And you don't mind being ignored?"

"These days, Mr Warrington, I largely welcome it."

"Why do I get the feeling that there is so much more to be discovered about the mysterious Miss Kathryn Barton?"

"And why do I get the feeling that you're not going to

be nearly as impressed as you think you are?" Kathryn laughed, feeling awkward to be stared at by the women, but curiously comfortable in his company. "It is not a happy tale."

"But still a tale I would like to hear," he said, whispering now as they neared her new workstation.

Kathryn immediately began to set up her work area, and Mitchell, sensing that there was no more they could say within earshot of everybody else, nodded his thanks before turning to walk away.

"Got yourself out of working with the yellow phosphorus for the day then, have you?" said a woman she recognised but whose name she did not know.

"Oh, *plus ca change, plus la même chose!*" Kathryn said, rolling her eyes at the woman.

"What?" the woman said, her mouth dangling open unattractively.

"The more things change, the more things stay the same."

"What's that supposed to mean?" the woman said, her mouth still drooping.

"Put simply, *'ere we bleedin' go again!*" Kathryn said, chuckling to herself at her very best East End accent. The woman's scandalised look wouldn't have been out of place in the very best of middle-class drawing rooms, and Kathryn found herself laughing out loud. Maybe she could learn to give as good as she was given.

CHAPTER TWENTY-SIX

*A*ll was silence when Kathryn returned home that evening. She had grown used to something cooking on the stove, something her sister had taken time to carefully prepare for her. Worse still, the place was in semidarkness. There was a single candle, lighting the main room, the candle on the low table next to the couch where her mother sat.

"Mama?" Kathryn said, taking an unlit candle from the kitchen table over to where her mother sat, lighting its wick from the one already alight. The gloom lifted immediately, and Kathryn knelt in front of her mother and took her hand, squeezing it urgently. "What's happening?"

"Oh, Kathryn," Beth said and smiled. "My dear girl,

are you home from work already? It seems only a moment since you left."

"Mama, it is almost seven o'clock in the evening, and almost dark. Where is Jane?"

"Oh, I think she just popped out to look for your father," Beth said matter-of-factly.

"I see," Kathryn said, patting her mother's knee before getting to her feet and crossing to the kitchen. She set the candle down on the table and sat in a chair for a moment, knowing that she would get nothing further from her ever-vacant mother.

Kathryn knew, of course, that Jane went out almost daily in search of their father. They had hardly spoken of it since they had argued, and she truly had no idea if this employee of Taylor and Scott would be able to help them at all. Of course, even if Warren Barton were found, he would still be the same man, the man who had left them behind. It was all beside the point... and Jane was never out so late on her own.

Whilst it was only seven o'clock in the evening, autumn was on its way and the nights were drawing down earlier and earlier. It was cold, too, and her naive younger sister was out wandering a world she didn't truly understand.

Feeling a sudden sense of panic, Kathryn, her cloak still fixed around her shoulders, set off in search of her sister.

It had just started to rain, the sound of it peppering the flagstones was almost therapeutic. It seemed to fit perfectly with the rumbling of carriage wheels and the clip-clop of hooves on the still-busy Kennington Road. She could hear the peal of the bell in the clock tower striking the quarter-hour as she sped north, heading for the river, retracing the footsteps she had only just laid down in coming home.

She was still on Kennington Road when she saw a girl running towards her. She recognised her, even from a distance. It was Jane, and although she was running, she was limping too.

Kathryn spread her arms wide as if to catch her sister, and Jane let out a bloodcurdling scream.

"Let me go! Let me go, I tell you!" she wailed and struggled like a wild animal caught in a trap.

"Jane! Jane! It is me! Kathryn, your sister, for

heaven's sake!" Kathryn held tightly to her sister even as she continued to struggle. "Jane, Jane, you are safe."

Finally, Jane stopped resisting and clung to Kathryn as if her life depended on it. Kathryn could feel her sister's entire body trembling. A cab driver drove his carriage past rather speedily, his horse whinnying in protest, and that everyday sound was enough to have Jane almost jump out of her skin. Kathryn began to feel afraid herself; what on earth had happened?

"Come on, let's get you home, you're soaking wet." She decided to wait until she had her back in the relative safety of their rooms before she questioned her. Gently, she led the shaking girl back through the dark streets.

The two of them almost fell in the door, wet through, with Jane shaking and crying. Kathryn immediately sped her through to the bedroom so that they could change out of their wet things. She worked quickly, hanging their clothes to dry in the kitchen near the stove, knowing that she didn't want to have to wear one of her better dresses to the match factory the following day. She returned to the bedroom to help Jane put on her nightgown. She noticed how she was covered in bruises and scratches, and how she tried to hide them.

"Oh, Jane, whatever is the matter?" Both girls started visibly when their mother appeared suddenly in the bedroom. "You are marked. What happened? Who did that to you?" She spread her arms wide and Jane, desperate for her mother, ran into them. "There, there, you're home now. You can tell me. You can tell your mama."

Despite the horrible uncertainty of the moment they were in, Kathryn could have cried with relief. Jane's obvious distress seemed to have reached Beth somehow, like a finger snap in her ear, shaking her back to the present moment.

"It's nothing, Mama, really," Jane said, unconvincingly as she gulped for every breath.

"Something must have happened, Jane."

"I was set about down by the bridge, that's all. It was a gang of those awful unruly, feral children that you see everywhere. They wanted money, and they weren't at all happy when I told them that I didn't have any."

"And they did this to you?" Kathryn asked, wondering at the scratches on her legs. Had some awful children really scratched and bruised Jane beneath her clothes? She shuddered.

"Yes, they were searching for money, even though I told them I didn't have any. They said I must have some hidden, and they were going to find it. But when they didn't find any, they just kept hitting me." Jane began to sob, shaking from head to foot, more distressed than Kathryn had ever seen her in her life.

Beth held her daughter tightly, stroking her hair until she was soothed. As Jane began to calm down, her mother lifted her chin and gently pushed her hair back from her face.

"Let's get you into your nightgown, shall we?" Beth said in a soft, motherly way that reminded Kathryn of the gentle, kind woman their mother had always been.

"I think I'll wash before that... if you don't mind? Those children were very dirty, and I think some of them were spitting. I need to be clean, Mama, I really do." Jane looked frantic again, ready to revolt if she were denied an opportunity to clean up.

"Of course, my sweet. You just sit down on the bed, and I will warm some water for you on the stove." And with that, Beth disappeared from the room.

"Are you going to be all right, Jane?" Kathryn asked. Something was niggling at her, something she couldn't quite get a grasp of.

"I will," Jane said in a flat tone.

"I know you want to find Papa, and I don't want to argue with you about it, truly I don't. But please promise me you won't go out so late again."

"I won't be going out like that again, I promise," Jane said, her eyes looking suddenly vacant, staring into the distance, reminding Kathryn of their mother's state over the past few months.

She could only hope and pray that she wasn't about to lose her sister to the same melancholy.

CHAPTER TWENTY-SEVEN

hen Kathryn felt a hand on her shoulder, she cried out in fright. She spun around, ready to fight. Her sister's attack of just two weeks before was still fresh in her mind.

"It's me!" Mitchell Warrington smiled uncertainly in the poorly lit Clerkenwell Street; his hands held up as if in surrender. "I'm sorry, I should have called out first."

"No, it's not your fault," Kathryn said, laughing nervously with relief, her hand on her chest steadying a thundering heart. "I was just in my own little world, that's all."

"I wish you didn't have to walk so far in the dark,"

JESSICA WEIR

Mitchell said, and then looked off into the distance, in the direction she was walking. "So, I thought you wouldn't mind if I walked with you for a while."

"You don't live this way, do you?" she asked doubtfully but smiled. This would certainly be a more pleasing end to a rather difficult day. But then, every day was difficult.

"No, but I used to. When I was a little boy, we lived down by the Elephant and Castle." He held out his arm, and Kathryn took it.

"*You?* You used to live down by the *Elephant and Castle?*"

"You look surprised."

"I am surprised. It's even more impoverished than where I live."

"And it's Kennington you live, isn't it?"

"Yes."

"It's funny, I always thought of Kennington and the Elephant and Castle as one and the same place. I mean, they sort of run into each other, don't they? It's hard to tell where one ends and the other begins."

"They are very similar."

"I think we lived there until I was about seven or eight."

"And then your family moved to somewhere better." It was nice to walk along with her arm in his, it felt very natural.

It didn't matter in that moment that she was just one of the match girls and he was the son of the wealthy factory owner. She had started to feel that these were the sort of things that didn't really matter to Mitchell. It was puzzling indeed, and she wished that she knew more about him.

"If my father weren't such a driven and ruthless man, my family would still be living at the Elephant and Castle. I would be the barely educated ragamuffin that I had already started to become, and my mother would still be scraping together enough food to keep us going. Well, if she were still alive, that is."

"You lost your mother?" Kathryn asked gently.

"Yes, she didn't really live long enough to enjoy too many of the spoils of my father's ruthlessness. I think we'd only lived in Holland Park for three years when she passed away. I was away at boarding school then. I wasn't even around to say goodbye to her." Although describing an event which must have transpired some years before, the look of pain on his face made it seem as if his tragic loss had occurred just yesterday.

"Oh, that really is so very sad. You must miss her, Mitchell."

"Yes, very much. She was the only warm human being in the family, the only one with a heartbeat."

"I am quite certain that *you* have a heartbeat."

"You are very kind, Kathryn, given that I am the wealthy son of the man who makes your working day almost intolerable. I live well on the back of your hard work, after all. I was well educated on the back of your hard work, of the hard work of women just like you."

"The fact that you seem to be uncomfortable with it tells me that you're a good man. Believe me, I know from experience that we do not get to choose our relations, our fathers."

"Ah, you have an awkward father too?"

"Yes, you could say that," Kathryn said and laughed. "You mustn't blame yourself for conditions at the factory. It's your father's factory, after all. He is the boss; he sets the rules."

"I don't think it's quite as simple as that," Mitchell said doubtfully. "Were it not for my father dragging his family out of the gutter, I could quite easily be working in a dangerous job with no provision for my safety."

"Is that why you spend so much time walking around where the lucifers are made? I have thought more than once there is no great need for you to keep putting yourself there."

"But the women are putting themselves there, aren't they? What sort of man would I be if I were comfortable with the hazards all around them and never once put myself in harm's way?"

"I understand what you're trying to do, I just hope that it doesn't mean you'll end up getting hurt." In her mind's eye, she pictured the woman who had once worked at Warrington's. The woman whose chin had seemed to disappear day by day, the woman who had been forced to work alone because her colleagues could not abide the smell of the shards of bone being ejected through her gums. She had an awful image of Mitchell's kind and handsome face being similarly disfigured, the lower jaw receding bit by bit until there was nothing left of it. She shuddered, and he stopped in his tracks, laying a hand on her upper arm.

"What is it?"

"Please don't risk getting Fossy jaw, Mitchell," Kathryn said with feeling. He was the only person in her world who currently showed her any kindness, the only bright light in the darkness of her days, and she had a terrible fear of losing him. She hardly knew him, but somehow his loss would be unbearable to her.

"I wouldn't want to risk being ill now that I know the only nurse I was hoping to come across at St Thomas's won't be there!" He laughed, making light of the situation.

"Have you always worked for your father?" Kathryn asked, suddenly wanting to divert the conversation from any talk of her old dreams. Part of her wanted to tell him that she longed to be a midwife now and so she would be little use to him. However, she would feel silly saying that out loud. Her dreams were unattainable, unreachable, what was the use in talking about them?

"I've only just finished my education. He wanted me to go to Oxford, you see, not for the sake of the education I would be getting, but for him to be able to say that his son had been there."

"But surely, he's proud of you?"

"I am bragging rights, nothing more. If he were proud of me, I would be working at a job of my choosing. But you see, Kathryn, whatever I achieved at Oxford was only ever going to end up being put to dubious use back at the factory. In the end, it was a pointless exercise."

"I'm sure that education is never really wasted."

"I must sound very ungrateful."

"No, not ungrateful, just sad, frustrated even."

"How good of you to see me as I really am." He smiled at her as they began to cross the bridge. "I must say, you are the only thing that makes going into that dreadful factory every day worthwhile."

"What a nice thing to say," Kathryn said and was glad for the darkness for she knew she was blushing terribly. "You know you can leave me here, Mitchell. If you walk over the bridge, you will only have to walk all the way back again."

"But I'm enjoying the company. Don't turn me away just yet."

"I wouldn't turn you away, and it *is* nice to have somebody walk me home."

"Good," he said, and his smile lit up his handsome face.

Deep down, Kathryn knew that it wouldn't do her any good to fall in love with this wonderful young man. There was no path for them, not with them living such vastly different lives. It would not be allowed. But for now, when everything else in her life felt so grey and miserable, she wasn't yet ready to let go of the feeling. She had already let go of too much.

CHAPTER TWENTY-EIGHT

"*J*ane? Are you all right?"

"Yes, I'm fine," Jane replied in the flat tone which had been hers for so many days now.

"Did Mama go somewhere?" Kathryn felt uneasy; she couldn't remember her mother going outside since the day they had moved into the shabby little rooms.

Kathryn was already used to the fact that Jane had stopped participating in family life altogether, although their mother seemed to have begun on a path of returning to them little by little.

Jane no longer had a meal on the stove when she returned home from the factory each evening, but Kathryn understood. Her sister had been badly beaten by a gang of rotten thugs and it was going to take some time for her to recover both physically and mentally. However, on that evening, a stew was bubbling gently on the top of the stove, and it smelled wonderful. So wonderful that Kathryn almost forgot her concerns for a moment as her stomach rumbled forcefully.

"Yes, she wanted to get some ale for the stew."

"Some ale?" Kathryn asked, her eyes wide, her voice incredulous. "But where from? Surely, she hasn't gone to a public house!"

"She said she was only going up to the window, Kathryn. She's taken a jug," Jane said with complete disinterest as if their mother leaving the house to tap the window of a pub and ask for a jug of ale was an everyday occurrence. Kathryn knew that such things happened, she had just never imagined her mother doing it.

At that moment, Beth Barton returned brandishing the aforementioned jug. She was wearing her good cloak and hat, which made her look all the more bizarre to be standing there with a stoneware jug filled with ale.

"Mama? You've been out?"

"Yes, Kathryn, I've been out. Twice today, in fact," Beth smiled warmly, and Kathryn felt her eyes fill with tears. Her mother was returning to her. "I got a little beef this morning for the stew. It's not much, but the butcher on Black Prince Road remembers me well and gave me a good price. As it was cooking, I got to thinking about the stews I used to have Mavis make for us; the beef and ale stew I used to like particularly and I think you liked it too."

"I did, Mama. I liked it very much."

"Then that is what you shall have, my sweet. You've been working hard all day, and my poor Jane is so out of sorts. You've been shouldering too much of this burden alone, and that is as much my fault as it is your father's."

"No, it isn't. It is every bit my father's fault not yours in the slightest."

"I am your mother; it was my duty to keep going for the both of you."

"And I am your daughter, and it's my duty to care for you when you have suffered. I was there with you that night, Mama, I understand why you couldn't face the world for a while."

"Are you crying?" Beth asked, and set the jug of ale down on the table before wrapping her arms around Kathryn.

It was the first time they had embraced for as long as Kathryn could remember, and she was almost swept away by the emotion. To have a parent back in the world with her, fully back, was more than she could ever have hoped for just a few weeks ago. It lessened that awful loneliness in a heartbeat, and she felt like a child again, even though she had turned sixteen the previous week. The first birthday of her life which had passed by entirely unmarked, not a comment made by anybody.

"I'm just relieved."

"I'm sure you must be. But I think we have another problem on our horizon now," Beth said and looked over her shoulder to where Jane was sauntering out of the room, presumably going to lay down on the bed where she seemed to spend so much of her time these days.

There was something about the way her mother looked at Jane that she couldn't quite fathom. It must be concern. "With our love and care, Mama, she will heal." Kathryn fought hard to ignore the fact that she didn't entirely believe what she was saying.

"When did you get so thin, my dear?" Beth said, still holding Kathryn against her.

"I'm still eating. Perhaps it is because I've never worked before in my life." Kathryn tried to laugh.

"Working, yes, but not doing what you wanted to do. I really am so sorry about all of it, Kathryn."

"It's not your fault, Mama. It's just life, and there isn't anything that we can do about it."

"Well, for now, the least I can do is feed you a tasty, hearty stew. After that, who knows where our fortunes lay?" Beth kissed Kathryn's forehead, and then gently released her.

CHAPTER TWENTY-NINE

"*I*'m afraid one of the woodcutting machines has broken down, ladies. The men are working on it, but you might be short of matchsticks for an hour or two." Mitchell Warrington threw a broad smile at the women. "I'm sure you all deserve a little respite from your hard work," he went on and gave the crowd of women working on the safer red phosphorus matches a conspiratorial wink.

Either his announcement or the wink, or perhaps even both, sent a little ripple of mumbled excitement through the room. For her part, Kathryn just wished that the little matchsticks would keep coming. She didn't want time to look up, time for the other women to look up. They already managed to be hostile when they had a full day, what would they be like with time on their hands?

Before he turned to walk away, Mitchell paused for a split second to lock eyes with Kathryn. He gave her a minimal smile, a smile which felt like their secret and then disappeared to tell the women working on the yellow phosphorus the same good news. Kathryn watched him walk away, fully expecting that he would bring the women working on the yellow phosphorus away from the area, choosing not to expose them for a moment longer than they needed to be exposed to that appalling viscous substance.

"I wonder what old Mr Warrington would think of his son slumming it with one of the match girls!" It was Mavis' voice. It was always Mavis' voice.

"Look at her, can't take her eyes off him!" piped up one of Mavis' lackeys.

"I don't think it's all one way, girls," added another. "I don't want to go breaking any hearts, but I think he was giving her a good look as well." This woman obviously didn't care whose side she was on, she just wanted to stir the pot. And it worked; Mavis' grey eyes narrowed, and the tiny woman looked fit to explode.

"No, what would he want with little Miss hoity-toity?" Mavis said, almost defensively. In that moment, Kathryn realised that her old kitchen maid harboured her own little dreams about the boss's son. If the whole thing wasn't so awful, she might have laughed.

"Maybe that's just the point," said the agent provocateur, not yet ready to stop stirring that pot of hers. "She's the only posh one 'ere, ain't she? Maybe he doesn't think he's slumming it exactly with one of her kind."

"She only thinks she's posh, Gladys!" Mavis said, almost spitting the words at the woman. Gladys, however, seemed rather more amused than dismayed. Well, a troublemaker she might be, but at least this Gladys wasn't afraid of the pint-sized mouthpiece that was Mavis Baines.

As it all went on around her, Kathryn slowed her work. She took extra care dipping the matches, not wanting to run out of the small slivers of wood and find herself with nothing to do but take part in so vicious a conversation.

"Well, she sounds posh!" Gladys went on, a look of pure mischief in her small, beady eyes.

Kathryn wished they would all just shut up.

"She ain't posh. Well, she ain't posh no more, anyway!" Mavis was like a dog with a bone. Clearly, the idea that Mitchell Warrington might actually like Kathryn was needling her dreadfully. "She thought she was posh when the old man was still at home, but he ran off and left them, he did. Probably shacked up with some other woman somewhere, someone with a bit of life in them, not like that cold, dead fish, Beth Barton!"

"Stop," Kathryn said, dropping the matchstick she was holding and glaring across the workbench at Mavis.

"Well, *she* thought she was something special and all," Mavis said, the bit firmly between her teeth now. "Quite the little lady in their terraced house on Cleaver Square. Don't live in Cleaver Square now though, does she? Your posh old mother living in two dingy rooms in Kennington. No better than she deserves, that's what I say."

"I told you to stop," Kathryn said, impervious to the curious stares she was receiving from all around her; all except Mavis, who seemed intent to blunder on regardless, immune to the signs of danger.

"He can't have thought much of you though, could he? That father of yours!" Mavis turned to look at her audience, a nasty, twisted smile on her face. "Up and left them, he did. Never a backward glance. Sold the house from underneath them, and now Miss hoity-toity has to dip matches with the rest of us."

"I told you to stop, Mavis Baines!" Kathryn said, hardly recognising her own voice it sounded so heavy with threat. Her hands were clenched into fists at her sides, and she felt every nerve in her body taut like a spring ready to let loose its potential energy.

"Best of all, there's them that reckon the old mother's gone mad! Hardly says a word now, never goes outside, not fit for anything but the madhouse. Get her sent to the Bedlam, that's what I say!"

Kathryn snapped. She barged through the line of tables which were butted together end-to-end. It was only by pure luck that a great tray of freshly dipped matches wasn't sent sprawling to the floor. Mavis stood with her mouth wide open, clearly shocked by the fact that Kathryn was moving towards her.

By the time she reached her, Kathryn didn't care about anything. She didn't care about her job, her future, even her life. She would stop Mavis Baines if it were the last thing she did. She towered over her, realising for the first time the great difference in their size. She had always known that Mavis was tiny, but she had never thought to use her own physical superiority to intimidate the hateful little woman. And intimidated she was, for Kathryn Barton's face was a study in pure fury. The rest of the women backed away. Mavis's lackeys could not be persuaded to put themselves in danger for her sake. Only Gladys kept close, the woman who didn't take either side. The woman who only wanted to see the whole thing descend into chaos.

"Now, wait a minute," Mavis said, her eyes darting away from Kathryn's relentless blue-eyed glare. "You know it was a joke. You shouldn't take things so seriously." Whilst her words seemed commanding, her voice seemed anything but. She was shaking, and it was affecting her vocal cords.

"A joke? To say such awful things about my mother? A joke? To constantly try to make my life a misery? Well, I've got news for you, Mavis, my life is so miserable that there isn't a thing you can do or say to make it worse. But I am tired, Baines, and I've got nothing to lose. I am sick to death of you, do you hear me?" Kathryn said, and gripped the front of Mavis' dowdy, well-worn grey dress. She twisted the material in her hands, hardly realising her own strength, for the motion drew Mavis closer to her and a little up on her toes.

"Wait," Mavis wailed, and there was a ripple of unspoken disquiet amongst the other women. No doubt there were one or two of them in the crowd who wondered if they might be next. Miss hoity-toity, the posh girl, was untested. They had never expected her to fight back, but now that she was fighting back, they were all wondering just what Kathryn Barton was capable of.

"Now listen to me, and listen well," Kathryn said, and in their little part of the factory, a pin drop could have been heard. "If you ever, *ever* speak to me like that again, Mavis, I will drag you through this factory and bodily throw you into the deepest vat of yellow phosphorus and hold you down until your ugly, wagging jaw falls right off. Is that understood?"

"Yes," Mavis said, her eyes darting this way and that, looking for an ally anywhere. Finding none, she was now as alone as she had always imagined Kathryn to be.

Kathryn didn't say another word, she just let go of Mavis's dress and gave her just enough of a shove to send her tottering backwards. And then, calmly, Kathryn made her way back to the disarranged tables, slotted them neatly together again, and continued with her work.

Trying not to smile, Kathryn realised that she couldn't remember anything being quite so gratifying ever before. It was as if the weight of the world had lifted from her shoulders, at least for a moment.

CHAPTER THIRTY

Kathryn had been hoping for a little longer in bed given that it was a Sunday morning. Even to sleep in until eight o'clock was a treat now for the young woman who had to rise every other day hours before the birds were singing in the trees.

However, at just seven o'clock, Kathryn was awakened by something which sounded like choking. She was instantly alert and sitting up on the couch, struggling to free herself from her blankets. It was well and truly autumn now, and just the weakest light was trying to break through the gloom outside.

The noise continued, albeit muted, and she realised that it was not the sound of somebody choking, but of somebody being sick. Feeling shaken by her sudden move from sleep to wakefulness, she searched for the small box of matches she kept on the side table with a candle on a saucer.

"Oh, sorry," came a weak and shaky voice when the match rasped against the side of the box casting a yellow glow.

"Jane? What is it?" Kathryn asked in a whisper, not wanting to wake their mother in the room beyond.

"I just felt so queasy. It was so sudden. It must have been something we ate last night." Now that Kathryn's eyes had adjusted to the gloom, she could see Jane kneeling on the rug, the bucket which Kathryn used for cleaning the floors in front of her.

"If it was something we ate last night, surely, we would all be sick," Kathryn said, and something which had lurked in the very furthest reaches of her mind for so many weeks began to make its way forward.

She closed her eyes and remembered her mother looking at Jane, saying they had another problem. Then she thought of the scratches and bruises on Jane's bare legs on the day she had claimed to have

JESSICA WEIR

been set upon by a group of ragged children looking for money. Even then, Kathryn had known. Kathryn had known that all was not as Jane was telling it. Too much did not add up, and yet she had so many worries, so much responsibility on her young shoulders, that she had subconsciously chosen to turn away from it.

"I'm sorry, Jane, I've let you down." Tears were already running down Kathryn's face; she was so certain she knew now what had really happened.

"You haven't, I'm just a little queasy, that's all." There was something in Jane's voice which proclaimed that she knew as well as Kathryn did that it wasn't just a little queasiness.

"What happened, Jane? What happened that night when I found you out in the rain?"

"I..." Jane began, and then her voice broke. A low and deep moan came out of her, a sound of the deepest despair. It was a sound that Kathryn had never heard before in her life and, as quiet as it was, it seemed to fill the room. It filled the room and bore down upon her, squeezing her, chastising her for not taking better care of her younger sister.

Jane collapsed to the floor entirely, her forehead on the rug, her knees tucked underneath her. Kathryn hurried across to her, moving the bucket, kneeling beside her and covering her sister's small, thin body with her own. She wanted to encompass her, to create a hard shell around her to keep her safe, but it was all too late. The danger had come and gone, and Kathryn had been too afraid to even wonder.

"I'm sorry, Jane. I'm so, so sorry. I should have been more caring. I should have been ready to listen."

"It's not your fault," Jane's words rattled out of her body, small and almost inaudible. "I couldn't say it, I was so ashamed."

"You can say anything to me. You can say anything at all, and I don't expect shame. You're my sister, and I love you. I know that whatever happened, happened without your agreement. The bruises, the scratches on your legs. I should have known. May God forgive me; I should have known."

"I didn't even know what was happening at first. It was so awful, so painful. I never thought he would do something so dreadful."

"Who?" Kathryn asked, feeling that sickening anger

bubbling up within her once again, the anger which had almost seen her strike Mavis Baines.

"He'd been so kind, so ready to help. And I really did think he knew where Papa was. He said he'd found him, that he was in some rooms by St James's Park."

"The man from Taylor and Scott?" Kathryn asked, her throat dry, her words a grating rasp.

"I truly thought he was telling me the truth. I'm so sorry, Kathryn. I'm so sorry that I was so stupid, so gullible. I just wanted to believe."

"You had to run all the way from St James's Park to Kennington?"

"I wanted to ask somebody to help me, but I was so afraid. Everywhere I looked there seemed to be grown men. I thought that they would hurt me too. I'm so afraid I cannot go outside; I cannot suffer that again as long as I live."

"I'm sorry, I'm so sorry," Kathryn said, her voice wavering as she cried. "I should have stopped you."

"You tried to stop me." Jane shifted beneath her, wriggling until she was upright, sitting back on her knees. "You tried at every turn to stop me. This is my fault, not yours," Jane said darkly. "You told me that no good would come of looking for our father, and you were right all along. I should have listened to you. You told me that I would find it out the hard way, and so I have."

"Oh, Jane, my dear sister, this is *not* what I meant," Kathryn said, sitting back on her knees too, a hand covering her mouth. "You cannot think that you deserve this. You were just looking for our father, that is all." Holding her sister close, willing the pain to transfer to her, Kathryn let the tears fall.

"You mustn't," Jane said in a whisper. "You mustn't wake Mama. She can't know, I can't tell her."

"But she's going to know sooner or later, Jane." Kathryn felt exhausted right down to her bone marrow, though she suspected that their mother already knew. Suspected that this was what had brought her out of her fugue. The question was, did Jane not know what was happening? "I think... I mean, I'm certain..." She couldn't say it, she just couldn't.

"That I'm with child," Jane finished for her, her voice

as flat as it had been for weeks and weeks, ever since the attack.

"So, you know?"

"I am fourteen years old now, Kathryn, I'm not a child. I'll never be a child again now, will I?" Kathryn could feel her heart-breaking at her sister's words.

"He cannot get away with this. We have to tell somebody. The police."

"They won't believe me, Kathryn, you know that. Even if we still lived on Cleaver Square, women aren't believed." She gave a brittle, mirthless laugh. "I am finally beginning to understand the cruelty of men. If I had recognised it in our father, I might not be here today on my knees wondering what on earth I'm going to do."

"I can't have you blame yourself. If he had never gone missing, you would never have gone looking for him. And if this man from Taylor and Scott hadn't been an evil, vile creature, if he had just helped you as he had pretended he would, then you would be safe. None of this is your fault. It is their crime, not yours."

"I think this is going to just about finish Mama completely, isn't it? Just when she seems to have been returned to us, I am going to send her straight back into that silent world, aren't I?" Jane's tears had dried, but she looked so forlorn.

"You leave Mama to me, Jane. You've suffered enough." Kathryn stood up and reached down to take Jane's hands. She led her across the room and settled her down on the couch that she had just vacated. She covered her over and tucked her in tightly, and then made her way into the bedroom to climb into bed beside her mother. She would wait for her to awaken and she would tell her everything.

CHAPTER THIRTY-ONE

*H*aving Mitchell Warrington walk her home had become something of a regular event. At least twice a week, he caught up with her before she was even out of Clerkenwell, and he always took her across the bridge and all the way along Black Prince Road. She allowed him to walk her along Kennington Road when he insisted, but only to within two hundred yards of her front door.

"One day you'll trust me enough to let me walk you to your door," he said one night as he walked slowly along Kennington Road, dragging the last part of the journey out as long as he possibly could. "I always stand here and watch you go in through your door."

"Then you know that I trust you, otherwise, I would

wait until you turned away." She was deflecting his curiosity.

"Don't think I don't know why you do that, because I do." He waited until she unhooked her arm from his, as she always did the closer they got to her home. As soon as she let go, he slid his hand down her arm and grasped her hand.

Kathryn felt like a thousand stars were shining brightly in her heart. His hand was large, warm, and the very feel of it was an unimaginable comfort to her.

"I know you probably have a very good idea how we live here, Mitchell, and the truth is that I am ashamed to have you take a step closer to it."

"You forget that I used to live at the end of this long road, Kathryn, at the Elephant and Castle."

"When you were a little boy, but not now. Now you live in Holland Park."

"I haven't changed that much. And you might not believe this, but I know what it's like to feel less than those around you. Do you know, when I was studying at Oxford, everybody knew my background? I mean, they're not just wealthy, they are upper-class... most of them. And believe me, those people can scent poverty a generation away. That's what my father never understood. He never understood that they looked down on me the way that he looks down on the people who work for him. That probably seems ridiculous to you now, suffering as you do at work in my father's factory. I don't know how else to explain it."

"You don't have to explain any further, Mitchell. It's possible for any of us to feel out of place where we are, wherever that might be. To be an outsider is a terrible thing. I'm looked down at the factory, not just by the bosses, but by the other women too. The bosses look down on me because they think I'm nothing, and the women look down on me because I've fallen from a privileged background. I've come to realise that the circumstances themselves don't really matter, for the feeling in your heart, in the pit of your stomach, that remains the same."

"You are too bright, too wonderfully intelligent, to spend the rest of your life dipping shards of wood into phosphorus."

"And if my father hadn't left us the way he did, I

wouldn't be. But the fact is that he is gone, he isn't coming back, and nothing is going to change. There's no point in my dreaming of a future I can't have."

"Don't let go of your dreams of being a nurse, please," Mitchell said, and it was as if the idea of it hurt him as much as it hurt her. "At least one of us has to end up doing what it is we were meant to do in this world."

"And what did you want to do, Mitchell?" Kathryn asked, expertly stopping him at the two-hundred-yard point, still set on having him not take a step further. However, she left her hand safely in his, not wanting to let go of him just yet.

But the truth was, soon or later, Kathryn would have to let go of him entirely. Sooner or later, her young sister would have a child out of wedlock, and through no fault of their own, the two sisters and their mother would be pariahs. As if things weren't bad enough. But even Mitchell, with his beautiful, handsome face, his open and honest heart, couldn't be expected to overlook that as well as her diminished status. However, she still had a few months, and she was going to cling to them as firmly as she held onto his hand now. She wanted to make enough memories to last her a lifetime.

"I've always wanted to be a teacher." He looked down at his feet as if he fully expected her to laugh at him.

"I think you would be a wonderful teacher."

"Do you know, you are the only person who has ever said that. My father sneered, and he's been sure to tell all the men who work in the offices at the factory of my little hopes and dreams so that they might smirk amongst themselves. I suppose he thinks that the more scorn that is heaped upon me, the less chance there is of me ever considering following my own path."

"Oh, Mitchell, that is awful. I know it is no consolation, but my father treated me much the same way. I've always dreamt of being a nurse, even when I was a little girl, and he never once encouraged me. He sneered, just as your father does, and belittled me every chance he got. I think it made me rather proud of myself that I held onto my dream nonetheless. Then after my mother lost her final baby... all I wanted was to help her and I knew in my bones that

I would become a midwife..." She paused for a moment and blinked back tears. "For all the good it did me in the end. I mean, he's won, hasn't he? I'm not a nurse, I'm a little match girl."

"Are you still studying? Are you still reading your biology books?" he asked hopefully.

"Even if I wasn't too tired, my heart isn't in it anymore. I might as well sit in the darkness every night wishing that I could be the Queen of England, for that is as close as I am ever going to get to nursing. But what about you?"

"I always wanted to teach in a free school, somewhere in this area, where I grew up. I'm very aware of the privileges I have, however much I might moan and complain that I'm not doing just exactly what I want to do." He shrugged and squeezed her hand. "The factory not only bores me, Kathryn, but it feels like the end of all hope. I don't mean for me, I'm well-compensated after all, aren't I? I mean, I look at the women, even the likes of Mavis Baines whom I can't abide, and yet I still pity her. It's the end of their hope that I'm witnessing, sometimes, even the end of their lives, and I feel complicit."

"You tell me not to give up on my dreams, Mitchell, but perhaps it's time to talk to yourself. Don't give up on your dreams, not when you have an education, a chance to do so much good in the world." Tears rolled down her face; ever since she was a child, Kathryn had wanted to do some good in the world. All she did now was provide lazy people with the easiest striking match it was possible to find. Who on earth did that help? It hardly even helped her.

"We will keep each other going, Kathryn." He looked around him quickly before pulling her towards him. He quickly wrapped his arms around her and gave her a brief and tight embrace. "If we can't keep our own dreams alive, we must keep each other's dream alive. What do you say?"

"I say you have a deal, Mitchell Warrington," she said and thrust out her hand for him to shake.

He shook her hand, and then raised it to his lips, kissing it gently.

The touch of those lips sent a warmth through her, igniting something, some small tinder inside her. Maybe there was hope.

"Go on then, run along home, Miss Barton, and I will

stand here and pretend I can't see you disappearing through your front door." He smiled his handsome smile at her and Kathryn could feel her insides changing, moving, swirling, as she spiralled, spinning through the air, falling in love.

CHAPTER THIRTY-TWO

"*R*ight, Miss Barton, you'll have to come with me!" Mr Harper appeared suddenly behind her as she worked with the dreaded yellow phosphorus.

Kathryn dropped the match she was holding onto the tray and turned to look at him. Mr Harper had such a look on his face that she felt instantly afraid. What on earth was this all about?

"Have I done something wrong?" she asked, her voice wavering with fear.

"Well, if that doesn't sound like a guilty conscience, girl, I don't know what does!" he said with a sneer and gripped her arm. "Right, to Mr Warrington's office with you!" he said and began to pull her along.

Stunned and terrified, Kathryn caught sight of Mavis Baines as she was dragged unceremoniously through the factory. Mavis gave her a lop-sided smile full of spite and self-satisfaction, and in that instant, Kathryn knew exactly what this was about.

After so many months of working in that awful place, Kathryn was to finally see the offices. Not only that, but she was finally to see old Mr Warrington close up. Both were things she would have happily forgone.

"In there with you." Mr Harper banged loudly on the door to Mr Warrington's office before opening it and pushing her inside as if he were a gamekeeper having caught a poacher on his master's estate. "Here she is, Mr Warrington."

"Thank you," Mr Warrington said, not even looking up from the paper he was signing on his desk. "That'll be all, Harper," he went on, dismissing his lackey without even a glance in his direction. What was wrong with these people? Those who clung to a bully, willing to put up with anything just to be by their side. Perhaps it was just fear, self-preservation, but whatever it was, Kathryn despised them for it.

Kathryn stood for several minutes in silence with her hands by her sides, trembling from head to foot. There was something of her own father about Mr Warrington, and she knew by instinct that this was by design. He wasn't busy, certainly not so busy that he couldn't deal with the girl he had specifically sent for. He was making her wait. He was letting her know that the sheets of paper on his desk held more importance for him than she ever would. She was nothing, nobody, and he wanted her to know it.

When he finally looked up, Kathryn's mouth fell open. How could he look so much like his son and yet be so very different? The same eyes, the same hair, albeit greying here and there. But those eyes, they were the same pale green, the same shape, and yet she realised, as she studied them, they couldn't have been more different. There was nothing in them but cold ruthlessness, scheming, like a barrow boy about to pick her pockets. Dead but alive all at the same time.

"So, you're the girl who somehow needs to be walked home every night, are you?" he said; his accent was working-class Lambeth, but his clothes were Holland Park. They were perhaps even more *Holland Park* than the natives. But then, he was a man who had clawed his way up from the gutter, a man who undoubtedly wanted everybody around him to know just how clever he thought himself.

Kathryn simply looked back at him, knowing that there was no point whatsoever in denying it. This man knew everything, and most likely also knew that she wasn't walked home every single night. Kathryn, however, could see a trap when one was laid down for her. He wanted her to say that his son only walked her home two nights a week, to fall into his trap so that he could feel even more superior to this stupid girl.

"Tell me, girl, is it just *you* who relies on the wages I pay you?"

"No, Mr Warrington. I have to support my mother and my sister," she said, in her finest Cleaver Square accent. The foul Mr Warrington wasn't the only one who could let those around him know just who he was. She was pleased to note that it certainly hit the spot, for Mr Warrington looked taken aback, studying her a little more closely for a moment.

"And where do you live?" he asked, seeming now more interested to discover more about the well-spoken young woman who worked for poverty wages in such hateful conditions.

"Kennington."

"Kennington?" he said and began to laugh. "Which end?"

"Closer to the Elephant and Castle," she said, and was gratified to see the flash of recognition in his eyes.

"And what happened to send you there, because it is clear you don't hail from there."

"The other end, Mr Warrington. Cleaver Square."

"You didn't answer my question."

"Is that necessary? To my work here, I mean?" She fixed him with her bright blue eyes. "Because what happened to me was out of my control. I had never expected to be responsible for keeping my mother and sister, and the details of how that came about are extraordinarily painful."

"You defend yourself rather sharply, don't you?" he

said and looked vaguely amused. "Looks like working here might have toughened you up."

"I think it was more than just working here."

"Well, now that my curiosity is satisfied," he said and looked her up and down. "I'll get to the point." He cleared his throat. "Stay away from my son, girl, or I'll toss you out of here. I'll toss you out and make sure that you don't get a day's work anywhere else in London."

"What?" Kathryn said, outraged. Not outraged that he had told her to stay away from his son but outraged that yet another man thought that he had the right to turn her entire life upside down as easy as clicking his fingers.

"Oh, I can see that you don't believe I have the power. Well, I have the money, girl. And haven't you heard? Money *is* power." His smile, which had it been kindly would have made him look just exactly like Mitchell, was cruel and predatory. No wonder his son couldn't abide him.

"Oh, I believe it," Kathryn said, feeling powerless, knowing that there was nothing she could do or say to beat this man. "Your son and I are only friends, sir, nothing more."

"At the moment, yes. I have no reason to disbelieve you. The problem is, you're in the gutter, aren't you? You want to get back to Cleaver Square, or at least you will if you've got any sense about you. And let me think, what better way for a girl fallen on hard times to get back to the glory days than find herself a fine young man from a wealthy family?" He raised his eyebrows. "But you want to know what the problem for you is there?"

"You don't know me at all, Mr Warrington."

"Well, I'll tell you," he went on, ignoring her response entirely. "I dragged my family out of the gutter years ago, girl, and I've got absolutely no intention of allowing my son to climb back in it with you."

She had never felt more humiliated.

Kathryn couldn't speak. She felt that vile anger and wanted to yell at him, to tell him exactly what she thought of him. She wanted to let him know that no amount of money would hand him an ounce of class for as long as he lived. She wanted him to know that his wealth didn't make him any better than he had been and that he would spend his entire life gathering more and more just to chase away the feeling of being less than everybody else. But to say these things out loud, to antagonise him, would be to find herself thrown out. She imagined that everything he had said about ensuring she received no proper work in London was true. He was ruthless, just as Mitchell had said he was, and she could almost feel his petty vengefulness. Yes, he would destroy her life if he wanted to.

"I can tell by the look on your face that we understand each other, girl." He smirked; he knew he'd won.

"Yes, we understand each other."

He looked back down at the papers on his desk, picked one up, and began to read it. He left her standing there, not knowing whether she was excused, not knowing whether she was expected to stay. Just like the beginning of their meeting, he was controlling this in every detail.

"Get back to work," he said in a low and dismissive voice without even looking up at her.

As she walked out of his office and closed the door gently behind her, Kathryn fought back the tears. That awful man had taken the last bright light in her darkness, and she would never, ever forgive him.

And she would never, ever forgive Mavis Baines.

CHAPTER THIRTY-THREE

*T*he next few months passed slowly for Kathryn. Every day, she saw the man she had fallen in love with on the factory floor, and it was beginning to drive her into the ground.

Mitchell had tried more than once to walk her home, only giving in when she begged him to leave her alone. She had only given him scant details of her interview with his father, leaving out each and every insult and doing her best to make it seem that his father, however misguided, had only his son's best interests at heart.

Mitchell hadn't taken it seriously at first, and so Kathryn had been forced to hurt his feelings, telling him that her job at the factory was more important.

She had cried herself to sleep for days and days afterwards. It had been one of the hardest things she'd had to do, wilfully turning her back on her only friend.

The only thing approaching a bright side was the fact that Mavis seemed to have given up trying to hurt her. In fact, she always gave her something of a respectfully wide berth, clearly worried that running to the boss to tell tales might have seen her thrown into the vat of yellow phosphorus just as Kathryn had previously threatened. The life went out of Kathryn that day as she had walked away from Mr Warrington's office, and she didn't have an ounce of fight left.

"I do worry about you, Kathryn," her mother said one day when Kathryn returned from work. "You used to talk all the time, you were so bright, so ambitious. Even working in that awful place, you still had your old fire in your belly. But now, it's as if it's been extinguished."

Beth was, as always, cooking something filling and nutritious on the stove. She had returned to her girls, it was true, but she had returned in a different way. She seemed somehow a much more substantial person than she had been when her husband had still been with her and the family lived at Cleaver Square. Beth had always seemed like a ghost, looking over her shoulder, trying to keep the peace, trying to keep her husband happy. Now, she was a much stronger woman, one who took care of everything inside their little rooms. She cooked, she cleaned, she did every stitch of laundry.

Kathryn knew that her mother was determined to be just that, a real mother. If only she still had Mitchell in her life, and if only her young sister wasn't growing bigger by the day, Kathryn knew she would have been thrilled, not just for her mother, but for herself also.

"Don't worry about me, Mama, not when we both have Jane to worry about." Kathryn lowered her voice to a near whisper even though her sister was resting in the bedroom.

"I must admit that I'm afraid for her. The *childbirth*, I mean," Beth said, and Kathryn could see that she was remembering her own failed pregnancies. "I know we don't really have much money, but I think we must pay a midwife to help us. I couldn't bear for something to go wrong and to not know how to fix it."

"I'll find somebody, Mama, and you're right, we do need help." Kathryn thought of Janet Baldwin, the dreadful midwife who had presided over her mother's last pregnancy and shuddered. If only she had been able to train. If only she was here to help her sister if she were some use, some real use in this life, not just a penniless match girl. "I'll speak to the doctor and see if he can recommend somebody."

"You are a good girl, Kathryn. Now then, sit yourself down, I managed to get some chicken for this stew." She gave her a motherly smile, and Kathryn felt briefly comforted by it.

It took only a few days for Kathryn to arrange a midwife to be called upon when Jane's time came. The doctor who had saved her mother the last time had recommended a young midwife whose rates were reasonable, and it gave Kathryn a good deal of peace of mind. Something was going to go right for once.

Kathryn had borrowed some books from the library, but they gave very little detailed information on the art of midwifery. She wanted to be ready to help when the time came, and she had found that the books, albeit they were not quite what she'd been looking for, had given her something to think about. She knew that her dream of being a nurse was as far away as ever it had been, but she had enjoyed studying again.

Thinking to return the books on a rare day off from the factory, she had decided to search the library for something with a little more detail. The Kennington library wasn't particularly well-stocked, but she left it with what she thought was the best of a rather lowly bunch of books.

"Miss Barton," a voice said rather firmly behind her as she stepped foot outside the library. "I'm glad I've seen you," the woman went on.

Kathryn turned to see Doris McCarthy, the young midwife, standing there.

"Oh, Miss McCarthy," Kathryn said and smiled warmly. The woman did not return her smile, and Kathryn felt entirely upended by it. "Is something wrong?"

"Yes, something is very wrong." Doris folded her

arms across her chest and raised her chin high in the air. "You didn't tell me about your sister's circumstances."

"What difference does my sister's circumstances make, Miss McCarthy?"

"I have a good reputation as a midwife, and I don't want anything to change that. And furthermore, I don't agree with young women running about all over town and doing just whatever they please without the benefit of marriage." Doris McCarthy had one of those accents that was neither one thing nor the other. She was a Lambeth woman, no doubt about it, but she tried very hard to appear not to be, and as a consequence, she had that rather ridiculous and strained way of speaking, that awkwardly proper way of speaking, which made her sound like one of the peelers of the Metropolitan police.

"So, you will only assist women if they come up to your standards?" Kathryn said, already bridling at the piety.

"I don't want to get myself a reputation as a midwife who will help any wayward girl give birth to a bastard." She lowered her voice to a near whisper, but she still drew the attention of an elderly lady who was making her way into the library. To Kathryn's surprise, the elderly lady looked furious, and turned away from the library to join them, uninvited.

"You're not going to get much work then, my dear," the woman said and laughed. "Not in Lambeth, anyway."

"What businesses is that of yours?" Doris McCarthy snapped.

"I'm only trying to help you, my dear. I worked as a midwife my entire life, right up until a year or two ago, and I can see you are heading for a fall, young woman. You're not a priest, you're a woman who ought to be helping other women. You don't get to decide who you will and won't help, not if you are a true nurse, and that's the truth."

"I have a right to my own standards!"

"Your own standards?" The elderly woman scoffed. She had a gentle accent, and she looked small and neat with her steel-coloured hair in a soft bun at the back of her head. She held her library book in one hand and a small open basket in the other. The truth was that she looked more like the sort of woman who might work inside the library rather than in the gore and shouting of childbirth. "Really, it's as if we don't all come into the world in the same way, isn't it? There's only one way to create a child and only one way to birth one. The sooner you put aside that crisp working-class judgement of yours, the better a midwife you'll be. In the meantime, I think it's fair to say that you're not fit to do the job." She turned to look at Kathryn. "Whoever the young lady in question is, she would be much better off without this woman."

"Thank you, Miss, but I really do need to find somebody to help my sister when the time comes." Kathryn was mightily impressed by this woman, but she was afraid that there would be no midwife to help Jane bring her baby safely into the world.

"Well, this book doesn't need to be returned until tomorrow." She tucked her book back into the basket. "What are you doing still standing there? Your help is not required any longer; begone!" she said sharply at Doris McCarthy who huffed and scurried away.

"Thank you for your kindness, for defending my sister and me."

"Think nothing of it, my dear. Now come along, Agnes Morland's tea shop might be a little scruffy, but she really does make the very best Chelsea buns. Let me treat you to one, and we'll see what we can do about your sister, shall we?"

CHAPTER THIRTY-FOUR

Gracie Hart was sixty-five years old, a retired nurse, and just about the most comforting person that Kathryn had ever met in her life.

Neat and small, she had such a presence that Kathryn couldn't have felt safer in the company of a man of six-feet-tall.

"How wonderful to have been a nurse," Kathryn said as she munched daintily at the Chelsea bun. "I always wanted to be a nurse. I had dreams of training at St Thomas's Hospital." How easy it was to admit her old hopes to this fine lady.

"And what is to stop you, my dear?"

"It's a very long story, but the short version is that my father abandoned us, and I am now forced to work in Warrington's match factory to keep a roof over my mother and sister's heads."

"Oh, dear, what a dreadful thing to have happened. What sort of a man abandons his wife and children? Really!" She tutted.

Kathryn was amused at this obvious display of disappointment in a man that Gracie had never met.

"Still, no point crying over spilt milk, as they say."

"I don't miss him; I don't even like him." Kathryn shrugged.

"Good for you!" Gracie said, and her lined face broke into a bright and admiring smile.

"Of course, none of that helps my sister." She leaned in to whisper, feeling so sure of this woman that she would have told her anything, any secret. "There was a man who worked in an office in London, Miss Hart, one who told my sister that he would help her find our father. My sister is only fourteen years old, and he didn't help at all. He was lying to her, and then he tricked her into a property in St James's Park and he forced her. He forced himself on her."

"The world is full of wretched men, my dear. Sometimes it seems that the only way to beat them is to keep going, to survive. It is often all we women have left to fight with. But then I suppose it is a good thing that we are so much stronger than they are, what do you think?"

"I think I am very glad to have bumped into you outside the library, Miss Hart. I wonder if I might ask you to help me further?"

"I already fully intend to." Gracie gave a confident smile. "And no, I'm not going to help you find some second-rate midwife who claims to have been trained, I think you deserve better than that."

"Oh?" Kathryn said, setting her Chelsea bun down on her plate and listening intently.

"I am going to help you to deliver your sister's child. You seem like a bright girl, educated, and obviously not squeamish if nursing is the thing you want to do. Now then, as you can tell, all my faculties are still in place, despite my great age, but my eyesight is a little wanting, and my strength has faded, albeit only a little. I shall oversee things, and you will help me. So, we'll finish our delightful Chelsea buns and our tea, and you can take me to meet your sister. We'll give her the good news together."

To be bossed around by such a capable older woman was just the ticket. Kathryn felt suddenly as if everything would be all right. If she could manage this one thing, everything else would fall into place, she was sure of it.

Fighting off the logic that this was a ridiculous sentiment, she determined to hold onto the feeling for as long as she could.

CHAPTER THIRTY-FIVE

*J*ane Barton went into labour in the middle of the night. Kathryn heard her cry out and dashed into the bedroom to find that their mother was already setting to work making her youngest daughter comfortable. Jane looked terrified, and Kathryn felt terrified too, remembering the night she had tried to help her mother give birth to the strangled baby boy.

"I'll go for Miss Hart," Kathryn said, already struggling into her dress and boots.

"Are you sure she will come? I know she's very kind, but she is elderly, and it *is* the middle of the night," Beth was whispering, not wanting Jane to hear.

"I know she will be here, Mama. She won't let us down."

Kathryn was right; Gracie Hart seemed to go from fast asleep to wide awake in the blink of an eye, and she was dressed and ready to go in just a matter of minutes. She picked up a bag which looked rather like a leather doctor's bag, that was kept right by the door. The fact that she was organised enough to be ready for that moment in advance was enough to restore Kathryn's confidence.

Although she had only been gone a short while, when Kathryn returned to their rooms with Gracie Hart in tow, it was to hear Jane crying out in pain.

"It sounds like she's already well on her way!" Gracie said with a curious bright-eyed relish. "Good girl! It won't be long now!" she called out to Jane before she had even reached the bedroom.

Jane was laying on her side ready to give birth in the genteel manner in which her own mother had been trained through many attempts.

"Oh, no, let's get her onto her back." Gracie was already rolling up her sleeves before tying an apron around herself. "Now then, Kathryn, are you and your mother able to lift that wooden trunk between you?" she asked, pointing at the ornate wooden trunk that the family had brought from Cleaver Square with all their clothes in.

"Yes, we carried it in here between us," Kathryn said and wrinkled her nose in confusion.

"Good, then if you would be so kind, lift it up onto the bed and lean it against the footboard. There." She pointed to where she wanted the thing.

Beth and Kathryn, both now looked confused but did just as they were told.

"Right, Jane, put your dainty little feet on that box. That's right, not on the top, on the side. Good girl, there is a method to my madness," she went on and laughed. "This will give you a way of bracing yourself when you need to push. No point trying to give birth side-saddle! It isn't a gymkhana!"

Jane lifted her feet and rested them flat against the box, her knees bent.

"Oh, that feels better already," Jane said and smiled.

"Now then, I hope the two of you don't mind me

doing a little ordering about for a while?" Gracie gave a bright smile to Kathryn and her mother.

"Not at all, Miss Hart, just tell us what you need," Beth said and rolled her sleeves up similarly, making Kathryn feel a great flush of pride for the mother who had once seemed so fragile.

"Mrs Barton, could you get some boiled water started?"

"Of course," Beth said, and instantly disappeared to the stove.

"And what about me, Miss Hart? What should I do?"

"Ah, now you, my dear, are going to deliver your sister's baby," Gracie said and gave Kathryn's hair a reassuring ruffle.

Jane Barton's healthy baby boy was born just as the sun came up on a cold but bright morning. She was exhausted, but she had coped with the whole thing so much better than Kathryn could ever have given her credit for. She was proud of her, especially when she saw just how much Jane already loved the tiny infant. She had put aside the awful circumstances of his creation and chosen to see him as her son.

Kathryn couldn't help but think of Jane's hopes and dreams, dashed even more than her own had been. Jane had dreamed of a perfect marriage, a fine home, a neat and tidy little family. There was nothing neat and tidy about any of this, and yet Jane's face, so full of love, couldn't have looked happier. Kathryn wondered if it was time for *her* to make the best of things, to see the good instead of always seeing the bad.

"Well, that was a night to remember, wasn't it?" Gracie said, looking pristine, and certainly not like a woman who had been awake all night helping to bring a child into the world.

"I can't thank you enough, Miss Hart," Kathryn said, and tears of gratitude filled her eyes.

The two women were sitting at the kitchen table drinking some well-earned hot tea. They were alone as Beth kept Jane and the new baby company in the bedroom.

"And I can't thank *you* enough, my dear. You putting

your trust in me has made me feel like so much less of an old woman. It has made me feel useful again, and I'm bound to say that it has perked me up no end." Gracie laughed.

"I was with my mother the last time she gave birth. It was the most dreadful experience, Miss Hart. The little boy died; he was strangled."

"It happens, and it is an awful tragedy, my dear. But so many births end like this one, happily, miraculously. As you go through your career, you will learn to accept the bad as well as the good."

"My career?"

"That's right, you heard me!" Gracie said, full of bossiness again. "Because I cannot possibly stand by and watch such a natural talent go to waste."

"Do you really think I'm a natural?"

"I would have given my eye-teeth to have been as confident and as capable when I was your age. You have a lot to learn, but I think you have a very good head start on all the others."

"You make me feel as if it's possible, Miss Hart. As if

I really might do my training at St Thomas's one day."

"Don't ask me how I know it, but I can feel it in my bones. And believe me, when an old lady tells you that she can feel something in her bones, it is always best to trust her."

CHAPTER THIRTY-SIX

Kathryn returned to her job at Warrington's match factory with a heavy feeling of trepidation. She had expected and had received, the most terrible dressing down from Mr Harper for having missed a full day of work on Friday and half a day on Saturday. She mumbled an excuse that she had been unwell and unable to let him know, for the fact that her sister had given birth was, in her opinion, absolutely none of his business.

In front of the other women, he had told her, in no uncertain terms, that if she ever failed to turn up again, if she was so much as late by one minute, he would throw her out.

Kathryn had made a good show of meekness as she

nodded and agreed, promising that it would never happen again. The truth was, however, that in the end, Mr Harper's harsh words had bounced straight off her. In terms of making an employee feel terrible, he was very much second fiddle to old Mr Warrington. She had fully expected to be dragged before him and was greatly relieved that Mr Harper had decided to deal with the situation himself.

As she set about her work, Kathryn wondered if Gracie Hart had been right, that she would one day be able to leave this awful place behind and take up her training at St Thomas's Hospital. Nothing had changed for her, and yet somehow, she felt buoyed up by Gracie's words. If that accomplished woman thought that she would one day do it, perhaps she really would.

Smiling to herself, she realised that Mavis Baines was glaring at her from across the workbench. Kathryn sighed and rolled her eyes before fixing Mavis with a stare of her own.

"Well? What is your problem this morning? Or are you simply peeved because you've got no more little stories to run to Mr Warrington with?" Mavis had grace enough to blush, especially since Kathryn had said it loud enough for her colleagues far and wide to hear. At the end of the day, nobody liked a tattletale. They might have despised Kathryn, but now none of them seemed to trust Mavis. After all, they might be next!

"That's right, there's nothing to tell anymore, not now that Mitchell Warrington has left!" Mavis barked the words, her voice full of accusation.

"What are you talking about?" Kathryn said, and could feel the edges being knocked off her good mood.

"Exactly what I said! Mitchell Warrington doesn't work here anymore. But then I suppose you already knew that didn't you?"

"No, I didn't," Kathryn said, with much less sharpness.

She looked back down at her work, hiding her reaction from the other women. It was true that she had hardly shared a word with Mitchell for some months now, but there had always been something comforting about the fact that she got to look at him now and again. Just to see him across the factory going about his business had slowly become enough for her. The bright light in her darkness might not have glowed as brightly as it once did, but it had still glowed. Now, that light was truly extinguished.

"Did you really know nothing about it, Kathryn?" Gladys, the factory pot-stirrer asked.

"No, Gladys, I didn't."

"Well, one of the other girls reckons that he had the most dreadful argument with his father. She said they were shouting so loudly at each other in that office of his that she thought they must've come to blows."

"Gladys, you're just making that up!" Mavis said, waspishly.

"Why? Why would I make that up?" Gladys went on, but Kathryn had to admit to herself, albeit begrudgingly, that Mavis had a point. Gladys was a troublemaker, one who liked to light a fuse and stand back a safe distance awaiting an explosion.

"What did they argue about?" Kathryn asked, wanting details, ignoring Mavis's interjection.

"She reckoned it was something to do with the factory. Looks like young Mr Warrington didn't really want to work here after all. Told his father that he was going to live his own life, that's what I've heard."

"You make it up as you go along," Mavis went on, determined to put an end to Gladys' telling of it.

"I'm not making it up. I heard that old Mr Warrington told him to get out and never come back. And that he shouldn't expect another penny from him either!"

"More like Mr Warrington threw him out because of her!" Mavis said, determined to embrace her own version of events. "I knew she wouldn't leave him alone. And now poor Mitchell Warrington has been cast out without a penny because of this selfish little rat!"

"I think I've warned you before about speaking to me that way, Baines!" Kathryn said, and gave Mavis a seething, threatening look. She was gratified to see that it had an immediate effect, even though the truth was she didn't feel angry, not in the slightest.

How could she feel angry when the man she loved had finally made his escape? He had stood up to his father, if Gladys was to be believed, and had decided to chase his own dreams.

"What are you smiling at?" Mavis said, although her tone was a good deal more respectful. "Do you think that you'll be able to get your claws into him now just because he's not under his father's gaze?"

"What business is that of yours?" Kathryn said haughtily.

"Well, good luck with that!" Mavis said and started to laugh. "He might have left his father, but he's still a respectable man. And what respectable man is going to want to tie himself to a woman whose sister has just given birth to an illegitimate brat?"

Once again, Mavis had the most up-to-date gossip, and Kathryn found herself silently cursing all of Lambeth for its small-minded judgements.

*a*s the day wore on, Kathryn's feeling of optimism began to drain away. It wasn't just an afternoon spent working with the yellow phosphorus and the fear which always came along with it, but Mavis's words had, in the end, cut deeply.

She was, and always would be, pleased for Mitchell that he seemed to have broken away from his father and she could only hope with all her heart that he would be able to maintain it and not find himself forced to return, cap in hand. But why should he fail? Why should misfortune continually befall him the way it had seemed to befall her in the time since her father had left?

Letting herself in through the front door of the terraced house her family shared with so many others, she felt a little stab of excitement. She couldn't wait to see the baby again, and wondered if her sister had yet found a name for the handsome little boy. She couldn't let herself think of how difficult his life would be without a father, or how difficult Jane's would be without a husband. It wasn't just the day-to-day provision of a good life, but rather the judgement and spite of others which left her fearing for the vulnerable little pair. But for now, he had been safely delivered, Jane had survived childbirth, and Kathryn knew that they had, in that if nothing else, so much to be grateful for.

Beth had firmed up dramatically, refusing all talk of giving her grandson up. She didn't care a jot for what people thought of her. Their friends had abandoned them long since; why should their judgement matter now?

"Where's that baby?" Kathryn asked excitedly as she bustled in through the door to their rooms. She quickly removed her little hat and cloak and hung them on the hooks beside the door, her nostrils filling with the scent of a wonderful stew. "I've been out of the house all day, surely, it's my turn to hold him!" she went on and laughed.

"I'm afraid you'll have to get in the queue, Miss Barton," came a voice she recognised. She sucked in her breath and turned sharply to see none other than Mitchell Warrington sitting at the kitchen table and cradling Jane's baby boy in his arms.

She closed her eyes tightly for a moment and then opened them again, fully expecting that she would come to her senses and the mirage of her handsome love would vanish. But he didn't. He was still sitting there, smiling up at her.

"Mitchell?" she said, her blue eyes wide, her mouth formed into a delicate, pretty *oh* of surprise.

"I was hoping to catch you this morning, outside the factory, but I had an interview."

"An interview?"

"It doesn't do a man's pride any good to realise that he hasn't been at all missed. You didn't even realise I wasn't there, did you?" he said and laughed.

"Of course, I realised," she said, wondering if this

was a wonderful dream that she was about to wake up from.

He must have been in the house for some time, for he seemed perfectly at his ease, as did her mother who had turned her back to them to stir the stew. There were already bowls on the table, dainty fine china bowls that they had brought with them from Cleaver Square. It had never occurred to her before that they looked so strange in that shabby little room.

"Gladys said that you'd argued with your father and left." She cast her eyes in her mother's direction, wondering if Beth was listening.

"Well, it's safe to say that, for once, Gladys was telling the truth." He laughed.

"Have you really left the factory?"

"I have." He looked so pleased with himself. "In fact..." His words were cut short when the baby boy in his arms opened his eyes, and then opened his lungs. He yelled, and Beth turned away from the stove, laughing.

"Oh, dear," she was smiling warmly, seeming to be enchanted with her baby grandson.

"I think he might prefer his mother to me," Mitchell said and gave Kathryn's mother a rueful smile.

"I think you might be right," she said and laughed, gently relieving him of the tiny, shouting baby.

Beth disappeared into the bedroom with the baby, and Kathryn took the opportunity for some hurried conversation with Mitchell.

"You went for an interview?"

"You won't believe it, Kathryn, but I am to be a teacher. I'll be working in a free school at the Elephant and Castle, no less!" He looked thrilled. "I will be able to give something back to the community that was once mine. What do you think of that?"

"I think your father must be furious," Kathryn said with wide-eyed admiration. "But I'm very proud of you. How brave of you to follow your dreams."

"Thank you. But now I think it's time for you to follow your own dreams."

"I'm not sure how possible that would be," she said and cast her eyes about the room. "As shabby as it is, it has to be paid for."

"Oh, I know," he said humorously. "I have one just like it."

"You have rooms?" Kathryn said, amazed. "You have left Holland Park?"

"I am your newest neighbour. Mr Richardson, and may I say what he lacks in charm he also lacks in decency, had a spare single room in this very building."

"You live *here?*" Kathryn said, unable to stop the smile breaking out. "Can you bear it?"

"It feels very familiar, I have to say. And to have my own space, albeit a small and dingy room, is more comforting than you can imagine. My father threw me out of Holland Park, of course."

"Because you decided to become a teacher?"

"No, because he finally told me exactly what he'd said to you that day, and I tore strips off him for the first time in my life. You see, I have become a teacher as a means of supporting myself. When I told my father exactly what I thought of him, that was when he decided that our futures were no longer aligned."

"Oh, Mitchell, I am so sorry. That is exactly why I

didn't tell you how your father insulted me. It didn't matter, you see. I mean, it hurt, obviously, but his opinion of me means nothing, not to me. You shouldn't have done that, Mitchell. Oh, I feel so dreadfully responsible."

"Responsible for what? Being the catalyst to have me finally take hold of my courage in both hands and follow my dream? Oh, yes, I think you should be dreadfully ashamed," he said and laughed heartily, that handsome smile of his lighting up his beautiful face.

"Are you really happy about it?" She looked over her shoulder and there was no sign of her mother. She had the distinct impression that she and Jane were listening intently from the other room, even though they made themselves scarce.

"I am happy that I was fortunate enough to secure a teaching position on my very first day of looking. I am happy that I have a roof over my head and some very fine neighbours. I must say, your mother is terribly hospitable. She has invited me to stay for dinner, no less."

"Wonderful."

"But more than anything, I'm happy to have you back. I do have you back, don't I?"

"Of course, you do. I am so sorry I had to turn away from you, your father threatened not only my job at the factory but my prospects of getting employment anywhere in London. It would have meant the streets for us, and what with my sister being..." She paused. She wondered if he had realised yet that her sister was unmarried.

"Yes, I can quite well imagine that the weight of your responsibilities rested heavily on your shoulders. But it really will all work out, you know. Your sister loves that child, it's very clear. Your mother loves that child, so your sister, unlike so many other young women, can be assured of her support. And now you have me too. If you want me."

"Of course, I want you. I can't tell you how hard it was to see you every day and not be able to speak to you. But even just your presence in the same building was enough to keep me going, Mitchell. You mean everything to me."

"Does that mean that you love me?" he asked, and there was a look of teasing on his face.

"Of course, I love you. I think you already knew that."

"Ah, but did you know that I love you too?"

"I didn't know it, but I had hoped." She felt tears in her eyes and Mitchell began to shake his head.

"No, no tears, no sadness. Just happiness and a determination to work together."

"I think that I could manage anything with you by my side. I could go to that factory happy every day if I knew that you would be here when I got home."

"Forget the factory," he said and shook his head. "I have great plans for you."

"Oh?"

"You are going to start your training at St Thomas's. I've already spoken to your mother about it, and she seems to think that some old dear called Gracie will know exactly what to do." He shrugged humorously. "So, that's that."

"I still need to..."

"No, you don't. You don't need to take responsibility for everything in your world. I will not allow anything to happen to your mother, your sister, or that nameless little boy. And your mother has already declared to me that she will seek a little employment of her own now that she's feeling so much better. You know, she really is terribly proud of you. She told me how you more or less delivered your little nephew on your own. She wants nothing more than for you to follow your dreams, and that's what I want for you too."

"I can't believe this is happening."

"Neither can I. Whoever would have thought that a blazing row could have made the world right again?" he said and peered mischievously towards the bedroom door before taking the opportunity to kiss her tenderly on the lips.

EPILOGUE

*I*t had felt like a very long night indeed, but it had been well worth the effort. The young mother, daughter of a wealthy academic on Baker Street, had delivered twins, both healthy, as was their mother.

The new father had cried with happiness, despite the presence of his stern-looking father-in-law, and a general sense of excitement and wonder had settled on the house. It had come as a great relief after the sad loss of a mother and child the week before. Kathryn hadn't been called out in time, given that she was not the midwife who had agreed to help the woman through. But realising that she was struggling and greatly out of her depth, Doris McCarthy, who wasn't as well-trained as she had once claimed to be, had panicked and called not only for the nearest doctor but for the best-trained midwife in the area. Kathryn Warrington, the midwife who had trained at St Thomas's Hospital, no less.

Despite hurrying, it was all over before Kathryn had even arrived. The woman wasn't her patient, but it affected her deeply nonetheless, it always did. She remembered how Gracie Hart had once told her that she would, one day, learn to accept the bad as well as the good, and she knew that she was coming to terms with such things as the years rolled by and her experience increased. It didn't help on this occasion, however, to realise that the woman lying dead was her old enemy, her old kitchen maid, Mavis Baines.

For all that Mavis had tried to hurt her in the past, the deep sadness that Kathryn felt was raw. She had stood in Mavis's bedroom and cried, much to the surprise of Doris McCarthy and the doctor. So, a successful birth was much needed, and whilst not an antidote to the sadness, it certainly helped take the edge off.

As she walked through the crisp Sunday morning air, she realised the rest of her family would already be in church. Well, babies came on their own timetable and nobody else's.

As she crossed Westminster Bridge, heading south, she paused. It was almost deserted, just like any Sunday morning, and it felt incredibly peaceful. The sunlight had that lovely yellow quality of early morning, and she saw it reflected like jewels on the surface of the water of the Thames. How pretty that dirty river looked on a sunny day!

Kathryn leaned against the rail, her attention turning, as it always did, to the immense building that was St Thomas's Hospital. She stared at it dreamily, smiling as she remembered all the highs and lows of her nurse and midwifery training. She remembered the kindness of her first ward sister, and the shocking sharp tongue of the matron who had presided for the entire five years she had worked there.

"Seeing you standing there like that reminds me of the first day we met," Kathryn was snapped back into the present moment to find her husband standing next to her. "That time you almost knocked me over."

"This is a nice surprise. Didn't you want to be in church, you miserable sinner?" Kathryn said and laughed.

"I walked down with the family, my love, and then I thought I might slowly make my way towards Baker Street and see if there was any sign of you yet. I must say, I'm glad you spared me such a long walk. How did it go?"

"Two beautiful, healthy baby girls." Kathryn smiled, her eyes shining with tears of emotion.

"You always look more beautiful when you've helped bring a child into this world, Kathryn," he said and gave her a loving kiss on the cheek.

"You do say the nicest things." She looked into her husband's faded green eyes and was taken back so many years to the day when she had collided with him on the bridge, not far from that very spot. She had been full of hopes and dreams then, and as her family had tumbled into disaster, she had never imagined that she would one day fulfil them.

Kathryn had continued to work at St Thomas's after her training, but she had found herself drawn more and more to the idea of specialising in midwifery.

After all her mother had suffered, and after helping Gracie Hart bring a beautiful nephew into the world, that idea had grown and grown until it had become irresistible. She had been nervous, at first, about making that move, but with Gracie Hart, still vital and bossy, ready to give her advice at any time of the day or night, she had grown in confidence until she had become just about the most popular midwife for miles around.

"You haven't forgotten that your mother has invited Arnold and Gracie for dinner this afternoon?"

"I had forgotten, but there's plenty of time for me to get a little sleep before then."

"Shall we walk? You look like you could tumble into bed and be asleep before your head hits the pillow." He took her hand and they continued over the bridge.

Kathryn loved Mitchell more and more every day. He had been true to his word, and from the moment she had found him sitting in the tiny rooms she had once shared with her mother and sister, he had worked hard to help her achieve her dream.

Joining forces with her mother, the two of them had

made it possible for her to leave the match factory and take up her training at St Thomas's after Gracie had put in a good word for her. And then, the incredible had happened. Just weeks after her training had begun, they were graced with the presence of Mr Arnold Wolverton once more.

He had come to them with what he had described as news which was both good and bad. Warren Barton had suffered a fatal heart attack quite out of the blue, and since his will had remained unchanged, everything that was his, everything that he had, in effect, taken from his wife in the first place, was now returned to her. He hadn't purchased another property with the money he had made from the sale of Beth Barton's childhood home, and so she largely inherited the lion's share of that money, rather than possessions.

Kathryn hadn't been surprised that Warren's passing didn't affect her, but she had been surprised that her mother and sister took the news without a tear. Beth said that, after what she had seen her daughters suffer, she didn't have a tear left to spare for the man who had caused it. As for Jane, her new life of motherhood had finally removed the blinkers once and for all, and she had come to see just what sort of man her father had been, and just how terribly he had treated her mother. To look at Beth and Jane now, nobody would ever suspect that they hadn't always been the closest mother and daughter in all the world.

"Is Jane going to help Mama prepare the meal?" Kathryn asked, already feeling sleepy and hoping that her mother wouldn't need her to show her face until it was almost time to eat.

"Yes, Jane and little William are going back with your mother after church. Roger has something to attend to, so he's going to join them a little while after. So, there's nothing for you to do, my love."

Jane, when the family had moved from the two rooms in Kennington to a neat, terraced house on Black Prince Road, found herself courted by an intelligent and handsome young man who lived on the opposite side of the street. Jane, far from the subservient woman she had been destined to grow up to be, had used the experiences life had thrown at her and had, much to Kathryn's amazement, become very active and vocal in the matter of women's rights. Roger, fresh from university and full of wonderfully open-minded ideas, had fallen in love with Jane in a heartbeat, and the two of them had married when little William was just two years old.

"Oh, how wonderful," Kathryn said and smiled when Mitchell squeezed her hand. "I don't think I was as tired as this even when I worked at the match factory."

"I think you might be remembering it rather differently," Mitchell said and laughed. "I, for one, feel exhausted just thinking about it."

Mitchell and his father had never reconciled, despite the fact that Mitchell had offered an olive branch more than once. It didn't affect him as Kathryn had thought it might; his father really had treated him no better than her father had treated her. And it gratified her to see how the relationship between her mother and Mitchell had developed so quickly and so well. He had found in Beth the mother figure he lost as a boy, and even as he had become more and more successful as a teacher, he had never pushed Kathryn to move out of her mother's home on Black Prince Road. Instead, they had lived there as husband and wife without any thought of leaving Beth behind.

Through all the adversity, the Barton women had held tightly to one another, and the family seemed to grow closer and stronger day by day. When things had been at their very worst, and Kathryn had felt herself to be alone in the world, she could never have imagined just how well things would turn out in the future.

"I do look back at those days, Mitchell, and I know how fortunate I am. I still think of the women who worked there, even the ones who were so cruel to me. I have been so blessed to be able to follow my dream, and to be married to the most wonderful man in all the world."

"I rather like compliments like that," Mitchell said and laughed. "But I do count myself very lucky too. I love you very much, Kathryn."

"And I love you very much." Kathryn smiled; there was mischief in her eyes, and she knew that it was time to tell him. "And I love this little one too," she said, laying a hand on her still-flat stomach.

"What little one?" he said, looking confused for a split second before reality dawned. "Do you mean...?" His green eyes opened wide, the smile spreading across his handsome face.

"I *do* mean." She squealed as he put his arms around her and then lifted her until her feet were off the ground.

"I'm going to be a father?" he said, setting her down on her feet and doing a little jump, tears shone in his eyes.

"Yes, you are going to be a father."

"Then I promise you, Kathryn Warrington, as God is my witness, I will spend my every waking moment striving to be a better father then either you or I were blessed with." His voice wavered with emotion. "And I promise you too, little one," he said, a single tear escaping his eye as he peered down, addressing her flat stomach.

"I have never doubted it, my love. You will be the best father in all the world."

Thank you for Reading

I love sharing my Victorian Romances with you and as well as the ones I have published, I have several more waiting for my editor to approve.

I would love to invite you to join my exclusive Newsletter, from it, you will be the first to find out when my books are available. It is FREE to join, and I will send you The Foundling's Despair as a thank you.

Read on for a preview of The Ratcatcher's Orphan

If you enjoyed this book please leave a review on Amazon or Goodreads, it will only take a moment and I would really appreciate it.

THE RATCATCHER'S ORPHAN - PREVIEW

"Sooner or later, I will have to speak to Mrs Coleman about this dreadful girl. Really, Rupert, this must be absolutely the last time we employ an orphan," Mildred Collins said in a whisper so loud that Jane knew she was meant to hear it.

"Did we ever employ an orphan before this one?" Rupert Collins asked, not even bothering with the pretence of a whisper.

Jane Ashford, the orphan in question and the maid in Rupert and Mildred Collins' home for almost a year, made a very good pretence of not hearing a word her employers said. Instead, she continued to build a fire in the grate of the drawing room. Her hands were shaking a little as she did her best to make a neat and symmetrical pyramid out of the coals.

To Jane, this seemed like a ridiculous, pointless waste of time. Why on earth would anybody need an unlit fire to look so perfect when, at any moment, they might strike a match and have the whole thing devoured by flames? It was just another quirk of the upper classes as far as she could see, and it strangely made her glad that she was not among their number.

Of course, being an impoverished orphan who had been edged out of the orphanage at just twelve years of age was not a particularly comfortable set of circumstances either. Jane had been picked by Mildred Collins. The woman's harsh glare had surveyed the short line of terrified girls, all of a similar age, in order to pick one whom she thought at least looked clean and decent.

Jane hadn't forgotten that day in the year and a half which followed, nor was she ever likely to forget it. She had felt like one apple in a box of apples at the market, with the prospective buyer studying her and all the rest at close quarters. At the time, she imagined being picked up out of the box and turned over and over in Mildred Collins' hands while the woman checked for blemishes. It had been a horrible experience, a dehumanising experience, and Jane had decided there and then that she would never like the woman. As the year had passed by and Jane had reached the great age of thirteen and a half, nothing had changed; she still did not like Mildred Collins, only now she had more and more reasons in her experience for that feeling.

"My dear Rupert, would you look at the dreadful state of those coals!" Mildred said in a high-pitched whine. "Really, it will be a mercy when the whole thing is set alight, won't it?"

"I never saw anything so shoddy, my dear, never." Rupert spoke in a somewhat deeper version of Mildred's whine.

Still, Jane knelt before the fireplace and continued to work. She felt humiliated, that dreadful sensation of being watched making her suddenly clumsy. Her hands were shaking with anger as she wondered if that awful couple had anything more in common between them than their cruelty.

"Girl, girl?" Mildred began in a determined tone. "Rupert, what is her name again?" she said in that *out loud but under the breath* way, a style that was all her own.

"It is Jane, isn't it? Yes, it is Jane," Rupert added.

Jane bit down hard on her bottom lip. They both knew very well what her name was, but this was just one more tool in their upper-class box; it was designed to dehumanise her further still. What on earth did these dreadful people get out of such games? Slowly, Jane turned her head.

"Mrs Collins?" she said in a respectfully enquiring tone.

"No, no, do not look at me!" Mildred said, her eyes lighting up with glee. "There, now look what you have done!"

Jane turned back to look at the fireplace and saw that the tongs she was using had knocked the carefully placed coals all over the grate when she'd looked around at her mistress. It made her suddenly angry; it was all so unnecessary. Why couldn't they have just left her alone to get on with her work in peace? But no, they had to irritate her, anything to get their little bit of sport. Well, if that was where they found their joy, at least Jane could be glad that she was herself and not either one of them.

"I'm sorry, Mrs Collins," Jane said with practised deference as she began to rearrange the coals.

"At this rate, it will be dark before the fire is lit!" Mrs Collins said as if this was the greatest problem life had ever thrown at her; perhaps it was.

Jane could hear the enjoyment in the foul woman's voice, and it was all she could do to stoically re-stack the coals. This little piece of enjoyment was also contrived, so determined, and it made Jane angry. So angry that she closed her eyes and imagined striking Mrs Collins with the tongs.

She imagined Mrs Collins falling backwards in surprise, her peculiarly peach coloured hair, hair which must once have been a much more vibrant red, entirely disarranged as the mobcap she wore about the house when they didn't have visitors flew off. The image amused Jane a little and was just enough to break the anger. Jane needed this position and knew that her employers were capricious enough to dismiss her for the smallest of crimes. Losing her temper enough to even mildly complain about her treatment would certainly be enough to see her out on the streets. If only any other household in all of London had come to the orphanage that day looking to hire a maid. If only everything didn't feel so insecure, so uncertain.

Of course, Jane Ashford wouldn't be the only servant in London who felt as if her position was insecure, she knew that was the truth. However, nothing felt steady to Jane in that house as her employers seesawed from cruelty to sense and then back again. But how would she escape them? If Jane were to leave and the Collins's didn't want her to go, Mrs Collins would simply not give her a reference. Jane knew that to have worked somewhere for more than a year and come out with no reference would make other households dubious of employing her. Oh, yes, Jane felt trapped all right.

Mr and Mrs Collins maintained their positions in the drawing room and watched Jane like hawks until the fire was finally set. Jane took a small cloth out of the pocket of her apron and wiped her hands clean before rising to her feet and getting ready to leave the room.

"Well, light it, girl," Rupert Collins said, shaking his head and tutting.

"Yes, sir." Jane reached for the box of matches on the mantle shelf. She struck one and lit the tag of paper she had left poking out between the coals. It was an easy lighting point. She gave it a moment or two before rising, seeing how well the fire took hold. She'd done a good job, whatever that miserable pair said.

"Will that be all?" Jane asked, her respectful tone so determined that it almost wasn't respectful at all. Still, she couldn't help but think that her privileged employers were too dull-witted to notice.

"Yes, that will be all," Mrs Collins said coolly.

Wasting no time, Jane hurriedly bobbed a small curtsy and headed for the door. As she reached it, she heard a clatter and a laugh and turned to see that Rupert Collins had used the poker in the fire to disarrange all the coals Jane had so painstakingly arranged. The laughter was Mildred's, clearly impressed by her husband's stupidity; what dreadful, privileged, pointless lives these people led.

"Would you just look at her, no better than she ought to be!" Mrs Coleman said with an angry click of her tongue.

Jane looked at her cautiously, then looked behind her. Mrs Coleman hardly ever spared her a word and certainly not in conversation. She gave her instructions, looked on disapprovingly, and that was that.

"Mrs Coleman?" Jane said in a quiet voice, certain that she must surely be mistaken; Mrs Coleman conversing with her? It was unheard of.

"Her, Miss Emma Talbot's maid! No better than she ought to be, I said!" She tipped her head in the direction of the window which looked out over the servants' yard beyond.

Jane followed her gaze to where a very fine-looking young woman was talking to Glyn Billington, the lad who delivered fruit and vegetables for the greengrocer.

Did Mrs Coleman have this right? The young woman certainly didn't look like any maid that Jane had seen before. Yes, she wore a dark dress, but it was nicely made, not the sort of thing Jane would ever expect to see a white canvas apron tied around. Her fair hair was in a bun, just as Jane's was, but there the similarity ended. She had little ringlets framing her face. Not so many as a fine lady might have, but it certainly seemed a little inappropriate for a servant. To top it all off, she was straight-backed and had a very obvious confidence about her.

"Are you sure she's Miss Talbot's maid, Mrs Coleman?" Jane asked, her curiosity giving her the courage to speak.

"Then you see what I do, Jane! No better than she ought to be!" Mrs Coleman said for the third time, and Jane wondered idly for a moment at the origins of such a ridiculous expression.

No better than she ought to be. It made no sense whatsoever, even though Jane knew exactly what it was meant to convey. It was a phrase she'd heard more than once as she'd grown up in the orphanage, a phrase that was designed to suggest that a woman suffered lax morals or was even a little promiscuous. Just as Jane was about to silently declare Mrs Coleman to be mistaken, she watched as Emma

Talbot's maid languidly reached out and took a shining red apple from the top of the box that Glyn Billington was carrying. The lad stood there simply looking at her, his mouth agape. The young woman was pretty enough, that was true, but not such a great beauty as to extract such an awe-laden response.

When the young woman bit into the apple, however, Jane felt her own mouth open. There was something provocative about it that she couldn't entirely explain, but there and then, she had a sense that Mrs Coleman might be right after all.

"Well, this won't get the house straight ready for the party, will it?" Mrs Coleman said with an uncustomary chuckle. "Right, Jane, I need you to check that all the guest bedrooms are fit and ready for tonight. I know they've already been done, but I don't want to chance it. I don't want one of the guests coming downstairs clutching a discarded polishing cloth like that dreadful vicar did last time!"

"Of course, Mrs Coleman," Jane said and darted away.

Jane crept about the upper corridors as silently as a cat, popping into one room after the other and carefully scouring each for any signs of forgotten cleaning materials. In no time at all, she was walking into the last of the rooms, having found nothing untoward thus far.

The final room was to be no different, although Jane lingered for a few minutes. This was to be the room that Emma Talbot stayed in, and Jane found herself thinking about the well turned out maid. The young woman was a lady's maid, of course, for that was the only type of maid who travelled with her mistress for a simple overnight stay. Lady's maids were always a little smarter, it was true, but that young woman might have passed for lower-middle-class, had it not been for that slight air about her. Had Miss Emma Talbot not noticed it? Or was it perhaps not obvious, something which the young woman had never let her mistress see?

Jane realised she was a little fascinated with the maid, wishing that she could work for an employer who would allow her better clothes, nicer hair. She tried to imagine Mildred Collins' reaction if Jane were to attend to her duties with her soft brown hair turned into ringlets at the front. She winced and shook her head; such a thing would not be tolerated; she knew that without a doubt.

Jane sighed and wandered over to the window, peering out over the rooftops and chimneys which pierced the pale blue sky. Not for the first time, Jane found herself wishing that she worked for anybody else in London. But perhaps not *anybody* else; perhaps somebody like Miss Emma Talbot.

The truth was, Jane, wished that there was another way to live, but people of her class, particularly orphans with no family to rely upon, had little choice in the matter. The whole system relied upon the existence of the poor, for who else would look after the seemingly useless rich? Jane didn't want to look after the useless rich, and she certainly didn't want to look after Mr and Mrs Collins. At night, she dreamed of a better life. Imagining that she had wealthy parents who had simply misplaced her, who had lost her through no fault of their own and had no idea that she had been discovered and placed in an orphanage.

She'd never known anything about her family, about the circumstances which surrounded her appearance at the orphanage as a baby. She'd asked, of course, but nobody had ever told her anything. The guardians at the orphanage were hardly any kinder than Mildred Collins, and Jane had always been told, as had each and every one of the other children, that she had likely been abandoned by a mother of loose morals. One who had enjoyed all the benefits of marriage without ever having spoken her vows. None of the spite stopped her wishing that she'd known her parents; her mother. It was like a gaping hole at the very core of her that would never, ever be filled.

"Well, this won't get the house straight for the party, will it?" she said, quietly parroting Mrs Coleman's words.

With a sigh, Jane turned from the window and wandered back across the room, taking a final look around to be certain that nothing had been left behind before she left the room and closed the door behind her

You can read The Ratcatcher's Orphan FREE with Kindle Unlimited

VICTORIAN ROMANCE

The
MILL DAUGHTER'S
COURAGE

JESSICA WEIR

The Lost Nightingale

The Ratcatcher's Orphan

The Orphan in the Blue Satin Dress

The Orphans Scandal

The Pickpocket's Christmas

You can find all my books on Amazon, click the yellow
follow button and Amazon will let you know when I have
new releases and special offers.

Printed in Great Britain
by Amazon

59641132R10190